Everlazt

Story by Author Everlazt

Cover by Author Everlazt

Copyright2016

To Lisa

Thank you

enjoy the read

EV...

DEDICATIONS

To my mom Jeanette Brown Josey and the rest of the Brown family, thank you for always holding me down. To my St.Thomas family, thank you for your support. To my sister…and brothers, Wastelandz we did it.

To my projects people's worldwide, I am your voice.

Be real and you shall win.

R.A.W.

REAL ALWAYS WINS

Prologue

As a light drizzle soaked the rotten apple, the stolen Jeep Cherokee rolled to a stop in front of building 57 on 160th street, between Broadway and Amsterdam Avenue. Everyone in the jeep had butterflies in their stomachs. That wasn't enough to stop tonight show.

"Check your watch Pee. We will be out of there in 5 minutes tops. When we go in, Sean you grab the money and drugs; me and Dre will hold the spot down." De'Quan said looking down at his watch. It was 4:47a.m.

"Pee give us to 4:52."

Pee nodded, and then set his digital guess watch, as his three passengers hopped out of the jeep and headed for the front door of the five story walk-up. They took the steps two at a time all the way up to the fourth floor.

De'Quan held up his hand to motion to Dre and Ne'Sean, as they caught their breathes. Then De'Quan eased up to the door and put his ear to it to listen for any sounds of movement on the other side. He heard a few voices that were rolling over the voices coming from the TV. De'Quan looked at Dre and Ne'Sean and nodded his head then pulled out his 40 caliber automatic. Dre and Ne'Sean followed suit by pulling out their own weapons and readied themselves for what was to come next.

De'Quan performed the secret knock he watched Melissa do earlier and took up his kick in the door stands, as Dre and Ne'Sean stood off to the side in anticipation. Suddenly an eye appeared in the peephole then quickly disappeared with the sound of the locks clicking from the other side.

Bolo snatched open the door surprised to see De'Quan there so late, "what do you..."

Bolo was cut off by the 40 caliber pistol which was shoved in his mouth with enough force to crack some of his

4

front teeth. Dre wasted no time as he pushed past them and ran into the apartment with the fire raging bull and his eyes, "Get the fuck on the floor Poppy!"

'It Started When We Were Young'

'From A Seed, Grew A Forest'

'How Strong Are Your Root's'

Chapter 1
1989

"Quan and Sean get your asses up and ready!" Mama K. yelled as she passed their open door on her way to the kitchen. De'Quan sat up and wiped the cold out of his eyes. He hated getting up in the morning more than anything in the world. At 12 years old, De'Quan already had a bad taste in his mouth for school. Once he learned how to read and count De'Quan began to get the feeling that everything else in school was useless.

"Sean, Mama K. said get up."

Ne'Sean rolled off the top bunk with an attitude and headed for the bathroom. Ne'Sean loved his brother but he covers De'Quan in his head as he walked by him. Just because De'Quan was two years older than him, that did not give him the title of ruler of the bedroom.

The bathroom door was closed, forcing Ne'Sean to knock on the door, "what is it?"

"Meika it's me. Come on I have to use the bathroom," Ne'Sean whined as he hopped from foot to foot.

The door opened up and Meika walked out the bathroom ignoring her brother as she headed for her room. Ne'Sean shot darts at the back of her head as he held his tongue and rushed into the bathroom to do his business.

De'Quan put on a pair of blue Levi's, a matching sweatshirt, and a pair of flis. Looking into the mirror, he began to comb his hair when Ne'Sean came back into the room smelling like toothpaste. Something the younger brother thought his older brother better go use, before going all up into Mama K. face this morning.

"Quan are you going to school today? Or are you going to that hooky party?"

Quan continue to comb his hair wondering the same thing. "What you know about that hooky party?"

Ne'Sean poked his chest out and said, "People got loose lips in these projects that are how I know about it."

De'Quan smiled himself and said, "Your right. That's gonna be a lot of these people down fall around here. Anyway you're not going. You my man is going to school."

"Why I can't go? I'll be in I.S. 205 next year. That just about makes me grown now."

De'Quan frowned, "look, if you miss school there gonna call here and top wheelchair bowlful of asses up. He'll know if you didn't go, then I damn sure didn't go to school. Now get dress so we can bounce."

Ne'Sean sucked his teeth and said, "Whatever, if I was you I would go sleigh that Dragon before you burn Mama K. eyebrows." They both laughed as De'Quan headed for the bathroom.

It was a slow morning and Marcy projects, the heart of Bed-Stuy Brooklyn, but Andre Jones was wide awake. He always felt best was the only way you were going to survive in New York City. Especially Brooklyn.

Andre was the same age as De'Quan and they have been friends since they were five years old. Andre waited in front of De'Quan's building thirsty to roll back over to the Flushing side of the projects for the highly anticipated hooky party. Andre lived on the Flushing side of Marcy projects and he could not figure out why De'Quan couldn't meet him in front of <u>his</u> building for change. Breaking up his thoughts was a burst of chatter from De'Quan, Meika, and Ne'Sean talking a whole bunch of nothing as they marched out the front door of the building.

"What's up Dre?"

Andre hopped in step with them and said," We have a little time to burn before we slide over there, so let's hit arcade."

"I didn't know junior high had an arcade in it", Meika said butting into the conversation.

De'Quan looked over to her and said, "mind your business and you'll live to see junior high".

"Oh yeah...

"You'll keep quiet regardless", De'Quan countered as he dug into his pocket for the $.50 anyway.

Dre snickered and said, "Meika you going to be one hell of a gold digger when you get older. You just got to switch your style up from ratting on everybody."

"Word" Ne' Sean added, as De'Quan just shook his head.

"Here, now poof- be gone!"

Ne'Sean and Meika crossed a street to go about their way, while Dre and De'Quan did a quick dip to the arcade. As 845 approached, they started to make their way over to the hooky party.

It was a Friday and everybody who was somebody from IS 205 was up in there. Tyshawn and his crew was deep in there, as well as Sabrina and her girls rolling hard. It was 40's of Old English being passed around, with bottles of Cisco, and some heads who where ahead of their time were smoking weed. Everybody wasn't ready for the Weed yet.

Around 11:30 am, the party was jumping. De'Quan had a Carmel complexion shorty in the corner of an already crowded couch. He was rubbing up on her half trained breasts and kissing on her neck when he heard a ruckus jumping off towards the front of the apartment.

De'Quan came up for air long enough to see Dre going at it with a kid from Tompkins projects. Dre was getting the best of the kid as he grabbed him by his shirt and swung the kid into the stereo. The impact scratched the record so hard the music shut off and a dark-skin girl barked, "What the fuck is wrong with yah!"

The few who were high off of the weed started to laugh, as De'Quan finally began to focus on what he was watching. He jumped up off of the couch and ran over to help out his friend.

B. Range came out of the back bedroom with a girl tight on his heels, "Yo man! What the fuck yah doing? Yah fucking up my mom's crib!"

At the end of his sermon, De'Quan picked up a lamp and smashed a kid across his face, because he looked like he was going to jump into the fight. At that site of this B. Range lost it, "Oh hell no! Everybody get the fuck out!"

Half of the party was already making their way out the door before he could finish his temper tantrum. De'Quan grabbed Dre by his shirt, as Dre continued to stomp on the kid.

"Yo man, let's get the hell out of here!"

Dre and De'Quan ran out the door and headed down the staircase, "let's go to my side of the projects where is safer. Them niggas won't come over there knowing my pops run that shit", De'Quan said in between breaths.

"Yeah, but what if your pops sees us?" Dre asked.

De'Quan thought about this for a second then said, "It's like 12 something now. So it's lunch time, he won't say nothing."

They walked over to the big park on the myrtle side of the projects, where damn sure enough pop was walking back from the weed spot taking a shortcut through the park.

Pop was a force on the murder which side that nobody really wanted to deal with. He stood at 6'1" tall with a golden brown complexion. His 175 pounds didn't make him as menacing as his temper did and that's what scared people. He met his chocolate sundae Mama K when they were young, and they had De'Quan shortly after a few episodes while his mother was at work.

Pop was America's nightmare. 30 years old, black, smart, and will kill to feed his family. Pop's soft spot had always been for his first born. De'Quan was Pop's mini-me when it came to him looking like his daddy. On the other side of the coin Ne'Sean and Meika came out as splitting images of Mama K.

Pop saw his son and Dre sitting on a bench across the park, oblivious to his approach from they're blindside. Pop smiled himself about the loyalty the boys had for each other. He knew that loyalty will run deep for some years to come.

"Aren't you two far from your school?"

Startled and mad at himself for not seeing Pop coming De'Quan said, "its lunch hour and we didn't want to be in the schoolyard, so we came to hang out in the park."

Pop just stared at them. He knew they were lying. He sidestepped their words and asked, "Dre why is your face all red with that scratch on it?"

Being a high yellow complexion, the slightest abnormality to his body will always show without warning. Dre looked over to De'Quan for help.

Pop said, "Yah were fighting, weren't you? You can tell me."

The two boys looked at each other again, causing Dre to speak up. "Pop, some cat from Tompkins's tried to front on me over a girl".

"Yeah so we gave them Marcy day", De' Quan added.

Pop laughed and said, "Yeah, well make sure you don't have that school calling me to come up there. You know I like to think in peace during the day." This meant enjoying his weed high without any disturbances.

Pop looked at his gold watch given them his silent signal it's time to go back. "Yah have any money?"

De' Quan reached into his pocket, "I've about $.70 left. What about you Dre?"

"I have a dollar left."

11

Dre was Pops son by another mother, as he liked to think of him. Dre father stepped off long before he could walk, making Pop the closest thing to a father he ever knew. Pop pulled out a knot of money and he peeled off two ten's. He gave one to each of them and said, "This better last yah until at least Sunday. Yah hear me."

The two boys nodded their heads.

"Now get back to school."

Boys quickly hopped off the bench and headed in the direction of their school, knowing full well they will not be going inside.

Chapter 2

That summer emerged as a hot one, with Ne'Sean graduating to the six grade. This Open the door for him to start hanging around De'Quan and his friends now. This did not sit too well with De'Quan, who just turned 13 and was feeling like nobody can tell him anything anymore.

At this point in his life, De'Quan was beginning to pay more attention to Pop whole style. To Quan, Pop was the most Gee up person in the world. When Pop spoke everyone who were supposed to listen- listened, even those who pretended to be minding their business.

Pop was grinding at a fast and heavy rate in the hot projects, as well as having control over a welfare hotel out in Queens. He made a new connection with some brothers down in South Carolina, and he was preparing to set up shop down there as well.

While Pop was out making the money, Mama K was holding down the home front and keeping the troops in line.

Meika stayed close to Mama K. Ne'Sean on the other hand started going out more and sticking with De'Quan and Dre, when they would let him.

On the morning of the first day of school, Ne'Sean was the first one up in the house. It was his day to start at IS 205 and his nerves would not let him sleep. By the time, he made it into the kitchen Mama K was getting ready for her morning rush hour. "Hey baby, what you doing up so early?"

"I couldn't sleep." Ne'Sean mumbled.

She smiled to herself. Another one of our babies was growing up. "Well I want you to learn all you can when you start 205 today, and be conscious of what's going on while you're learning. Because they teach us a lot of things in schools that isn't always true. Something like a bent up truth. I'm going to let you in on something that you won't learn in school. The Indians discovered America." She winked her eye at him and he laughed.

"You don't believe me?" Mama K asked.

"I believe you Mama K. I knew something was funny because they kept saying Columbus ran into the Indians when we got here", Ne'Sean said cheesing.

"Good. Always remember things we learn can be researched. Now go get cleaned up, and get dress."

"Yes Mama."

De'Quan was still in the bed dreaming when Ne'Sean walked into the room. Watching his brother's sleep, Ne'Sean thought to himself, 'I should do something to him now, because he's going do something to me later being that his freshman day'. He went into the bathroom and grabbed the toothpaste. Easing up on his brother Ne'Sean sprayed some toothpaste on his pillow, than began to snicker as De'Quan rolled his face over into the glob of toothpaste.

Watching his brother smear toothpaste all over his face Ne'Sean could no longer hold it and burst out laughing. Mama K began to come down the hallway barking orders into the rooms to wake up her little troops. When she walked into the boy's room, she saw what Ne'Sean was laughing at and smacked him in the back of his head

"Quan get up!" Mama K yelled, walking over to the window to raise the shade. She let the sunlight and could not hold in her own laughter, as De'Quan rubbed the toothpaste across his face.

"No... No, don't touch the bed", Mama K said.

"What the hell." De'Quan blurted out once he began to realize what was happening.

"Don't you cuss in this house? Now go wash your face," she said with a chuckle.

Ne'Sean stepped to the side with a smirk on his face, as his brother mumbled, "you'll pay for that."

"I know Colgate."

$$*****$$

Ne'Sean made it school without incident, then coolly eased his way into his first period class. He took a seat in the back of the class and looked over to the kid that was sitting next to him. He recognized the kid from the playground in Marcy. "What's up, my name is Ne'Sean."

"What's up, my name is Jamel. You from the Myrtle side of Marcy, right?"

"Yeah, building 105. What building you from?" Ne'Sean asked.

"Building 101. My brothers are the Moore twins." Jamel answered.

"Okay, I've seen them around."

the back wall. Then he pulled some money out of a sneaker box in the hole in the wall. Pop made sure, when he had this stash spot put in you would never know was there. Unless he showed it to you or you started kicking the whole wall out. He counted out 30,000 cash, put it in the Nike plastic bag and put the rest of the money back in the wall. Then he picked up the phone and dialed out a number he had gotten out of the newspaper a week earlier.

"Hello, Miller rentals".

"Yes, my name is Ryan Short and I'm interested in the store front on Lewis Avenue and Green Street that is up for rent. I was wondering can I take a look at it with someone that's in charge of its sale".

"Yes...Yes Mr. Short. I can make an appointment for you to meet with the building owner...aww...hold on a sec".

When he returned to the phone Pop said, "I'm sorry, who am I speaking with, so I'll know who's putting this together?"

"No, I'm sorry. My name is Bill Conners, and I've found the owner information for you. I will give him a call and take care of all the arrangements for you two to meet. Let me have your day and night time numbers so we can reach you please".

"Ok. 718-555-3572, if I'm not in, then you can leave a message with my wife".

"Okay, we'll do".

When he hung up the phone, Pop put on his bullet proof vest, polo knit sweater, and his black leather jacket. He grabbed his 16 shot 9mm, checked it, and then slid it in his inside jacket pocket. He put on a black ski hat, grabbed the Nike bag of money and headed out the door.

When Pop stepped out into the cold winter air he found himself thanking God the snow stopped coming down. He trekked over to the pay phone on the corner of Nostrand ave and Park ave. He dropped a quarter into the phone and dialed a number he knew by heart. A deep accented voice came over the line after two rings.

"Ola?"

Recognizing the voice, Pop responded, "This is Pee. I need to see you".

The man said, "Ah Pee. My friend. Come see me at 4:00".

"Ok. I need to see two mommies today", Pop said.

"Si. I have the perfect sweeties for you", the man said, then hung up.

Pop walked down to his parked 300E Mercedes Benz shoveled the snow out of his way and off of his car. Then he peeled out and headed for the weed spot and Bushwick.

He checked to see if anybody was following him several times, but he did not see anything unusual. He decided since the store was in Queens and he had about two and half hours to burn, he should go to his down low chicks crib on the Corona side of Lefrak City, and hang out there until 4 PM.

As he waved through traffic on the Interboro Expressway smiling to himself on how more and more his plan was beginning to look better as the day went along. He was going to buy two keys of Coke. Stash one and give the other one to his lieutenant Uni. Pop can tell Uni he had other things that needed his attention and to just bring him back $40,000 off of that key. Uni was a good worker and very reliable. He'd jump at the chance to prove himself without Pop breathing all down his neck.

His next step would be to get the building owner to rent him the store front. Then he came get Mama K to help him build up the store's clientele. He didn't like her working as a nurse attendant, but she always said it kept her busy.

He stopped at Deidra house on 57th Ave, at 2:40 PM. As usual, she was ready to smoke some weed and fuck. He caught the time at 3:55, and he couldn't afford to be late. He jumped out of Deidra and told her to keep the pussy warm; he'll be back distasteful smell of coffee, rolled off his breath and smacked Mama K in her face hard enough to let her know he had been having a long night. So she got right down to business.

"I don't have a lot of time, so can you please explain to me what's going on with my husband", Mama K said, looking around at her surroundings.

Detective Kelly thoughts himself 'get a load of this one'. "Well, your husband is in Kings County hospital right now under arrest. We have been following him for some time now and when we tried to arrest him today, he opened fire on us. Shot one of my offices and I'm not too happy about that. When the confusion was over Mr. short was still conscience, but he was shot three times. I believe he's alive because he was wearing a bulletproof today.

"Now, while he is in the hospital he won't be allowed any visitors until he's moved to a more secure place, even though he's up and in stable condition. He gave me your number and asked me to call you."

Mama K sat there soaking it all in, then asked, "Well what is he being charged with?"

Detective Kelly took a sip of his coffee and said, "At the moment attempt murder on a few officers, weapons possession, and drug possession".

"You can't tell me this over the phone? I mean – being that you're saying I can't see him without you being a part of our conversation. So, what's the real reason for the getting me out of my bed at three in the morning Mr. Kelly?" Mama K I asked with a slight attitude. Pop had taught Mama K not to panic if a situation like this ever occurred. Just take charge, and don't trust the police.

"We were hoping you might want to help your husband out here. If you look at the bigger picture your husband is in a lot of trouble right now, and any information you might have for us..."

She cut him off, "Listen Detective, you're barking up the wrong tree. I don't have any information about nothing but children's school clothes, and attending to old people who's, sex life been over years ago".

He said, "Come on Mrs. Short. You expect me to believe you don't know anything about the drugs your husband has been pushing to kids and…"

She stopped him again, "Look, what did I just tell you? Now you are insinuating things in my direction, and I'm not comfortable with this line of questions. Which is giving me the impression I'm going to need a lawyer".

Talk of a lawyer threw the Detective off. Usually he would have cracked a dealer wife by now. The thought of him being in the station for the last 14 hours crossed his mind and he made up the decision to shut this interview down. He was too tired to tussle with this one right now, but he had to take one last shot at her.

"I'm just trying to give you the opportunity to come clean about your husband's dealings, because the bottom line is, in the long run, we can charge you with accessory to his dealings".

She chimed in, "Well, I'm not being charged tonight for shit. If I were, I would be over there in that cell. So if you're done, I would like to go now".

He gave up and pulled out one of his cards. Handing it to her, he said, "Only if you change her mind".

She took the card and got up without saying another word. Stepping back out into the cold night the wind blew harder enough to carry the Detectives card up in the air as she flung it into the night sky.

came. "Docket number 3577/91, people v. Short. He is charged with attempt murder (four counts), possession of 2000 g cocaine and possession of a weapon and the first and second degree."

Without looking up the judge asked, "How does the defense plea?"

Mr. Schollof spoke, "The defense pleads not guilty Your Honor".

The judge looked up real quick from the paperwork he was reading to look at Pop. Pop looked like he was in a lot of pain carrying his cast and bad leg at the same time across the room.

Mama K put her hand across her mouth to stop herself from screaming. To her Pop looked like a wounded bird. He had a deep limp all the way to the table, and he was wearing a pair of dirty sweatpants she had never seen before. A hospital gown and hospital slippers rounded out his outfit for his late-night appearance.

"Bail?" The judge asked looking in the ADA's direction, who jumped right into his sermon about how Pop, was a threat to society, who was facing some serious charges, and therefore should get nothing but three hots and a cot.

"Your Honor, my client is seriously injured and we are axing for bail to be set at $50,000. This way my client can receive medical care from his personal doctor upon making bail."

The judge looked at Mr. Schollof and said, "Counselor, you're not serious right? Your client tried to kill four police officers. There won't be a bail ahead at night. Remand! Next case."

With that said Pop turned around and caught eye contact with Mama K, before he was led back into the belly of the beast.

Chapter 6

Mama K left the court feeling defeated. She thought she would at least hear a bail that wasn't outrageous enough to break them... She was still debating on what to tell the children as she drove back home. The boys were old enough to understand, but Meika will be a problem. By the time she got home, it was 9:37 PM, and Kim was trying to put the kids to bed. He heard Mama K come in and it was like that energy took on a new level. Meika ran up to her and of their saying, "Mama K, I want a piece of cake."

Mama K looked over to Kim, and Kim said, "She won't go to bed tonight if she eats another piece of sweets."

Mama K looked down at Meika and smiled, "Oh yeah, so we had our sweets for the night already."

De'Quan wandered over and asked, "Where's Pop at Mama K?"

Mama K had made up her mind the car. She was going to keep it real with our kids and tell them what happened. She needed their strength right now, just like they needed her strength every day.

She said, "Everybody come here in the living room and sit down. I have to tell you something."

All of her little troops and Kim filed into the living room. De'Quan, Ne'Sean, and Kim sat down on the big leather couch, Meika sat on Mama K's lap on the loveseat. She began with, "I don't know how to tell y'all this, so I'm just going to come right out and tell y'all. Pop is in jail-"

De'Quan jumped up stunned, cutting her off, "What!"

"Please sit down." She said, but he didn't so she continued. "He also was shot really bad. He's okay though. I saw him tonight at the courthouse," she said with as much's composer as she can muster without crying.

"Mama K can we go see him to?" Meika asked before anyone else could.

"Yes of course baby," she said. "I have to go see him tomorrow and find out what's really going on, because honestly I don't know why he's in jail or what happened."

After sitting there in silence, Ne'Sean looked like he was at the point of crying. Kim noticed this then put her arm around for comfort. "When is he coming home?" De'Quan asked.

"I don't know when he's coming home baby, and when I go see him tomorrow, I'll find out when we can go all go see him, and if we can bring him stuff", Mama K said as she looked from face-to-face to give them some assurance.

"Can I sleep which shoots and night Mama K? I'm scared", Meika asked with tears forming in the corner of her eyes.

Mama K wiped because face with her hand and said, "Sure baby. Now come on y'all is time to go to bed."

Kim took Ne'Sean hand and used the other one to guild De'Quan as they gave Mama K a hug and made their way down the hallway to their bedroom. Once the children were in the bedrooms, Mama K and Kim met up in the kitchen and sat down at the table.

"Damn its times like this when I needed a drink." Mama K said. They did not keep any alcohol or drugs in the house, because they knew how kids love to experiment.

"What you need me to do?" Kim asked. She reached out to hold her cousins hand across the table.

"I'm going to bring him some clothes tomorrow and see what's up. He looked so sad and hurt tonight. I don't want the kids to see him like that", Mama K said.

Kim said, "Damn, what about his bail? What did they say? You know I'll run up on *Uni and them, and tell them to get that money up. Speaking of which Uni and Rock called here a few times tonight wanting to know was going on? I told them whenever they know is what I know. They said they'll call back to see what's up."

"Those motherfuckers won't even give him a bail." Mama K said rubbing her eyes as she continued. "I'll deal with Uni and them when I speak to Ryan. I'm going to need you to hold me down tomorrow while I am at Brooklyn house."

"What time are the visits?" Kim asked.

"I'm going to call tonight before I go to sleep, so I'll know what my day is looking like while the kids are at school. If anything, I will call you in the morning. You going out tonight?"

"No. Trevor is coming over later. I ain't got my freak on in like a week." They chuckled, which somewhat relived Mama K. Kim continued, "Anyway, I might hang around here for the next few days."

"Would you", Mama K said feeling touched.

"You know I got your back girl. Tomorrow I'll bring some clothes over." They stood up and hugged. "Don't worry; it's going to work itself out."

Mama K put on her strongest smile of the night and said, "I pray that your right."

Chapter 7

Pop was lead back through the doors after losing the battle of trying to get a bail. Handcuffed and disgusted, he was taken through few underground tunnels over to Brooklyn House of Detention. There he was processed and given an I.D. number. Pop didn't make it to a cell with a sleep-able bed until three in the morning. By that time, the doctors had fed him with enough pain killers to make Pop pass out as soon as his head hit the hard mattress.

8:00 in the morning the cell doors popped open, waking Pop up to pain all over his body. He brushed his teeth, swallowed a few pain killers and stepped out of the cell. Pop looked down the fifteen cell gallery from seven cell, and then slowly made his way down the gallery to the dayroom area to use the phone.

"Damn! You alright homie?" A dark skin brother asked, as he looked up from the morning paper.

"I've seen better days. Anybody using that mic?" Pop asked.

"Naw, go ahead."

Pop picked up the receiver and dialed his house number. Mama K picked up on the second ring, "Hello?"

"What's up Mama?"

She jumped up from her seat at the table, "Oh baby, are you alright?"

"Half and half. Listen I need some clothes. Them…"

She cut him off, "I know. I just sent the kids to school and I was just about to call up there again to see when I could come up there and take care of all that."

He tried to get comfortable as he leaned up against the wall and saw there was a visit schedule taped next to the phone.

"Oh shit, here go a schedule right here. It says I can get a visit today from 1 to 9."

"Okay. Let me get my stuff together and I'll be up there by 3."

He said, "Alright, we'll talk more then."

"I love you Pop."

"I love you too K", and they hung up.

"Yo Black, let me talk to you for a minute", the dark skin brother said from his seat at a round plastic table large enough to seat four. Pop limped over to the table and grabbed a seat looking from the guy who called him to a Latino kid with long brides.

"What's your name?'

"Pop."

"Ok. Ok. My name is Shabazz. You want a cigarette?"

"Yeah." Pop took the out stretched cigarette, lit it, took a long pull, and slowly sat back in his seat as he released the blue smoke into the air.

"Yo where you from?" Shabazz asked.

"I'm from the Myrtle side of Marcy projects. Where you from?" Pop asked.

"I'm from Brownsville. Yo, as a matter of fact, you was on the news for the last two nights, right?" Shabazz said.

Pop let out a slight laugh and said, "Shit you know more than me. I went from K.C.H., to central booking, then to here in like 48hours."

The Spanish kid final spoke, "Yeah that's him. Yo, my name is B.R., and I'm from Williamsburg." He gave Pop a pound.

"Damn, I heard about you holding down Marcy. I got some wears for you if you need some things", Shabazz said, looking Pop up and down.

B.R. chimed in, "Word. I saw a new nigga come in last night rocking a Polo outfit that will fit you."

Shabazz and Pop burst out laughing.

"Naw, I'm good. I'm going on a visit in a few hours. I just need to lie down and get my head together. My body is mad sore."

"I bet you are. I got some soap and eats for you. You don't have to pay me back or nothing", B.R. said.

Shabazz said, "Here hold down this pack of cigarettes".

Pop gave both of them a pound. "Good looking", he said, then slowly got up and made his way back down the gallery to seven cell.

* * * * *

Mama K called up Kim and told her what time the visits started. Kim felt relieved it wasn't in the morning, because she was still in the bed recovering from her late night rodeo show with Trevor. Kim told Mama K she would be over by noon to prepare to receive the kids when they came home.

When Mama K got to Brooklyn house, it seemed like déjà vu from the night before at the court house. The line was full of wives and family members, all with the same tired and stressed out look on their faces like her.

Pop walked out onto the visit floor and it seemed like all conversation stopped for a moment. He put on his hardest gangsta bop he could muster to mask the limp he was walking on. Mama K stood up with a bright smile, hugged him and kissed him. As they sat down, she bit on her bottom lip to stop herself from crying. With his good hand, Pop moved the hair away from her eyes and smoothed her cheek.

He broke their silence, "How did you like my gangsta lean just now".

She smiled and shook her head, "Damn Pop. What the hell happen out there?"

He sucked his teeth and said, "Mama K, I thought them niggas were stick-up kids, or some dudes trying to hit me up. I didn't know they were cops. When I shot the first one, they just rained down on me from everywhere. God was definitely watching over me."

"I spoke with Schollof and he told me you might not get a bail or anything. How do you want me to pay him? And what about Uni and them, they called last night asking me what's up?"

He said, "I'm going to get the price from Schollof when I speak to him in a few days. The money Uni has for me, tell him to give you half. That's 25thou. You use that to pay Schollof. In the house I have…"

She cut him off, "I know. I counted it and took it to Moms house, and I found some more over there. "

"Good. That money is our future. All together it's close to 90gees, maybe a little more. That's got to hold us down until we see what's going to happen with this case. Tell Uni with the other half of the money he can do what he feels, that's on him. Between me and you, this is our out. Out of the Game. I've had enough. These crackers might try to hang me behind this shit. I just hope Schollof can pull a rabbit out of his hat." Pop said feeling weigh of a heavy career on his shoulders.

She said, "I brought you enough clothes to last you a few days and I put a $1,000 in your account. The kids want to come see you too. "

"Bring the kids next time you come. Remember Mama K, it's just us now. Once you get that dough from Uni, all of our street ties are severed as far as money is concerned. That's why that dough was in Moms house. With that, you're going to have to flip it on a legal tip. Just until I can come home and help you out, okay?"

A tear rolled down her cheek and he caught it with his finger, then he kissed her on the forehead. "I know it's going to be hard, but remember it's been just me and you since before De'Quan was born. We can do this. Just be strong, okay?"

"Yes", she answered.

"Table 12, your visit is over. Say you're good buys", A chocolate c.o. barked from her chair across the small visit room.

Pop said real low, "I got to go babe."

More tears rolled down Mama K's face as they stood up and embraced. "I got you, and I love you."

They kissed and he said, "I love you too." Before walking off with sadness in his eyes.

Chapter 8
De'Quan

Pop was locked down now and being the oldest sibling in the house De'Quan felt a little weight on his shoulders to step up. If not now, then definitely in the near future. De'Quan knew he was next in line to become the man of the house at 16, and there were moves to be made. How to start is where he was lost at.

De'Quan was going to Grover Cleveland high school, on the border line of Brooklyn and Queens. The school was like no other to him. Nobody went to class that wasn't important to them. The strong aroma of chocolate ty hung heavy in the bathrooms. The staircase is where the robberies went down at if you weren't on point, and the coolest females hung out in the lunchroom for at least 2 periods in a day if they weren't outside in the school park.

De'Quan had a small crew now consisting of Dre, Fat Pee, and a dark skin brother named Rahkem, who was bigger than his age of 16 suggested. Rahkem wasn't one of the flyest guys in the school, but Dre liked his style, so they put him down with them.

Q was the other new edition to the crew, who was a pretty boy from Jamaica Queens. De'Quan liked him because Q gave him some competition when it came to bagging girls in and outside school. They like going at each other on who could get the prettiest girl for the week, and the bonded from there.

All five friends were standing on the back staircase, smoking cigarettes, and talking a whole bunch of nothing when the question came up, "Yo Quan, what's sup what your pops?" Fat Pee asked.

De'Quan blew out some smoke and said, "He's alright. They're still trying to sort through the bullshit. They saying he might be on the island for a while".

The boys jumped up and made their way down the hallway with Ne'Sean in tow. When they made is safely into De'Quan's room Fat Pee was the first one to speak.

"Yo man, what gives with Mama K sniffing us like that?"

"Sean come here", De'Quan said. Ne'Sean walked over to his brother as everyone else watched in silence. De'Quan blew his breath into Ne'Sean's face without warning.

"What the hell you do that for?" Ne'Sean asked with a frown on his face.

"What my breath smell like?"

"It smelled like peppermint dummy", Ne'Sean asked irritated with the ginny pig exercise he was just put through.

"What you think she smelled?" Dre asked.

De'Quan thought for a second, and then said, "I don't know. Mothers are strange people man. Forget that, let's wash our hands and go eat. I'm starving".

Once they finished eating De'Quan said, "Mama K we going downstairs for a little while."

"Yah be careful. Quan I want you back up here no later than 11:30."

"Ok Mama", he said as they walked the door.

Mama K and Meika were cleaning up the kitchen when Ne'Sean put down his video game and came out his room looking to follow his brother and his friends. Without turning around from the sink Mama K said, "Where do you think you're going?"

He stopped in his tracks. 'I almost made it', he thought to himself.

"I'm going downstairs with De'Quan and Dre".

"No you're not. You're going back into that room. It's already 9:00 o'clock, and you have no business down there. Go find something on TV and we are finished in here we'll come in there and watch it with you".

"But Mama K", Ne'Sean whined.

"Boy what I said", she snapped.

Ne'Sean knew it was time to get out of dodge. He sucked his teeth, turned on his heels and moped back down to his bedroom.

De'Quan stood in front of Dre and Fat Pee who were sitting on the bench in front of De'Quan's building. A light breeze moved through the project court yard as De'Quan looked around a few times before pulling out his pack of cigarettes. He gave one to Dre and lit up his own. Fat Pee didn't smoke.

"De'Quan what's up, you said you had a plan. So what is it?" Dre said.

De'Quan lowered his voice where only the three of them could hear him, "I got a place we can rob". He stepped back and watched their reaction.

Fat Pee said, "Rob? Shit man, I thought we was going to sell drugs out here".

"Word, what gives Quan?...I mean the whole Marcy respects Pop, and I know we can get some crack heads on the strength of Pops name. People out here know you not going to sell them no bullshit, so we can get sales". Dre said as Fat Pee nodded in agreement.

De'Quan took a pull on his cigarette, blew out the smoke, and said, "Listen that's the problem right there, the whole projects know us. I don't trust people out here anymore. Somebody told on Pop, and we still don't know who did that. Shit, we set up shop and motherfuckers tell on us cause we getting Pops clientele. Then we be right on the Island with him. I'm not trying to see that".

"Shit, neither are we", Dre said. "We don't even have a gun, and what's the place anyway".

Chapter 9

Saturday

Click…Click.

Ne'Sean heard the sound, but he thought it was his subconscious mind playing tricks on him. He rolled over and felt movement in the room. Lying on his stomach, Dre slowly open his eyes, and began to focus on the figure sitting on the bottom bunk.

"What's that?" Ne'Sean asked in a groggy voice.

De'Quan was startled by his voice. He quickly tossed the gun under his pillow and blurted out an angry, "Go back to sleep man".

"Let me see", Ne'Sean pressed, hopping down from the top bunk.

"Look, I told you to go back to sleep", De'Quan snapped.

"Man it's time to get up any way, and I'm not a baby or stupid Quan. I saw the gun. Let me hold it".

Thinking about what to do next, De'Quan looked at the door as if he didn't already lock it and push the dresser on it. He picked the gun up and said, "You better not tell anybody I let you hold this. Not even Jamel".

Ne'Sean's eyes lit up, "I swear I won't tell anybody".

De'Quan made sure there weren't any bullets in the cylinder, then handed it to his brother. Ne'Sean held the gun lost in his own world for a moment. He cocked the hammer, pointed the gun at the window and pulled the trigger. When it clicked, De'Quan spoke and moved on his brother at the same time, "Man give me that".

"Why you snatch it like that?" Ne'Sean asked clearly upset about what just happened.

De'Quan said, "Stop asking so many questions. All you need to know is if something happens to me, and Pop doesn't come home, then you are the man of the house you dig. Then you will be able to carry one of these".

"Let me go with you", Ne'Sean asked out of nowhere.

De'Quan chuckled, "Go with me. You don't even know where the fuck I'm going".

"Where you going then?"

De'Quan ignored his brother, put the gun and bullets in one of his sneaker and slid it under the bed. "Don't touch that gun again unless I say so, you hear me?"

Ne'Sean sucked his teeth, "yeah I hear you". Feeling disappointed, Ne'Sean moved the dresser from in front of the door and headed off to the bathroom.

De'Quan went out into the kitchen and found Mama K in there making pancakes and sizzlen, "Good morning baby".

"Morning Mama K, did Dre call yet?" He asked, sitting down at the table.

"No. Where yah going so early on a Saturday?" she asked.

"We might go down to Fulton Street to hang out then go over to Fort Greene to play some ball" he answered.

"Yah be careful out there", she said moving toward the ringing telephone on the kitchen wall. "Hello. Morning Dre, hold on".

De'Quan hopped up and grabbed the receiver, "What's up...ok...yeah I'll be ready in 10 minutes. Yea she's cooking," De'Quan said loud enough for his mother to hear.

"Tell Dre I'll make a plate for him", Mama K said as Meika wondered into the kitchen rubbing her eyes.

"Come through, she said she got you", he said then hung up.

"Meika, you all up in that refrigerator like you brushed your jibs already". De'Quan said, taking an early morning shot at his sister.

"Shut up! Mama tell him to leave me alone". Meika whined.

"You do look like you missed the washcloth on your trip to the bathroom this morning, with all that cold in your eyes. But, you still my baby- come here and give me a kiss". Mama K said with a big smile on her face.

De'Quan just shook his head and walked out of the kitchen, "Unbelievable Mama K".

                *****

De'Quan, Fat Pee, and Dre hit Fulton Street by 11 o'clock to pick up their ski mask from the army and navy store. Then they stepped in Dr. Jays to buy three sets of black Nike gloves. Once they finished picking up their supply's the boys walked over to Fort Greene projects to play a few games of basketball.

"A Yo...we got next", Dre barked as they crossed the court and headed for the bleachers to change into their b-ball gear.

"Check it out, the police make their rounds at 9:40p.m. We go in there at 9:50p.m. on the dot, and we're out of there in 3 minutes", De'Quan said. He looked up from tying his shoe to see if they had any feedback.

"So which way we gonna run too when we come out?" Dre asked.

De'Quan said, "We run to Marcus Garvey, than make the left and try to jump in a cab, since Pee won't be able to make it back to the project on foot".

Dre laughed and Fat Pee took offense, "Fuck you Quan, I ain't that slow".

"Ok, my bag", De'Quan chuckled, than he got back down to business. "The meet spot is Dre's crib, cause he's the only one with his own room and his moms is hardly there".

"That sounds cool", Dre said nodding his head in agreement.

"NEXT!" Someone yelled from the basketball court.

"Ok…now let's go bust these niggas asses", Fat Pee said as he hopped off of the bleacher and they took to the court.

* * * * *

Mama K took Ne'Sean and Meika up to Rikers Island to see Pop, while her oldest son hung out with his friends on this clear and sunny Saturday. Prison officials made Pop status C.M.C. (captain escort) because of his case and all of the publicity it was drawing. Pop was being held in N.I.C. (north infirmary clinic), on the high security third floor until his trial.

Mama K did not mind coming to visit Pop while he was in N.I.C. because she only had to wait 15 minutes after she was processed to see him. Compared to the horror stories she heard from other visitors having to wait for an hour or more to see people in other buildings on Rikers Island.

Mama K loved to style on the female c.o.'s whenever she came to see her husband, like she was doing on this busy Saturday with her Gucci skirt suit and matching loafers. The hateful stares she received walking through the steel gates spoke volumes to Mama K as she ignored them and helped her two kids through the process.

Meika wore a pink Gap skirt, a white Gap sweater and pair of pink Reebox sneakers, while Ne'Sean rocked a stonewash

54

Chapter 11

Stepping onto the visit floor on a Wednesday night always felt electric to Pop. Wednesday and Thursday night visits on Rikers Island were usually resevered for the wives or the baddest girl friend a prisoner had, and they always came dressed to impress.

Mama K lit up as usual when Pop was escorted into the visit booth. She stood up, embraced and kissed her husband. All of the tension Pop had in his body from being constantly on point flowed right out of his body and he was ready to sit with his family.

Pop turned to his left and locked eyes with his oldest son and smiled, "What's up champ".

De'Quan beamed as he gave his father a hug. Mama K usually went up to visit Pop by herself on Wednesday and Thursday nights, but De'Quan missed the last visit and asked to take the ride with her tonight.

"What's up Mama?" pop asked with a look of concern in his eyes.

"Ain't nothing. I'm just tired", she said as she reached out across the table to take his hand.

He took her hand and said, "I know…we all are tired." Pop looked over to his son and said, "De'Quan why you so hard to catch now a days?"

For a moment, De'Quan got nervous. Sometimes you didn't know what Pop had on his mind, or if he already knew you were doing wrong behind his back. Pop always had eyes on his children in the projects and De'Quan knew the eyes had be out extra hard now that Pop wasn't out on the streets to watch for himself.

"I be around the building or on the other side with Dre and them. When you getting out Pop?" He said to change the subject from him.

Pop looked from De'Quan to Mama K and said, "They offered me a better deal. I called my lawyer today and he said they are offering my 7 ½ to 21 years. I told him I will have an answer for him by my next court date. What do you two think?"

Mama K gently closed her eyes, than open them. "That's a long time Pop. But, it's better than the time they're saying you going to get if you lose at trial".

Pop looked at De'Quan and said, "Can you hold your mother down for me for 7years?"

De'Quan stuck his 17 year old chest out and said, "Yeah Pop".

Pop smiled and said, "Mama I know it's a long time, but I'm starting to look at this situation realistically. I got caught at the scene with a smoking gun in my hand. I'm not going to beat that. Even in Brooklyn Supreme court they'll find me guilty of something, and I already have a year and a half in on the island".

"All of that time counts right", Mama K said to make sure.

"Yes it counts. So this is what I want yah to do. Open up that store front. The one I was looking at when I was home is still on the market. Put it in your mother name as the person leasing and financing it. That way welfare won't be sniffing around asking where you got the money from. Me and your mom already spoke to the owner of the property and it's going to cost $1,300 a month to lease it. Have you been reading those books I told you to read on how to get the candy and food from the vendors?"

"Yes, and I spoke to a delivery company that will give me a good deal on the newspapers. The boys and Meika will help me clean it up and stock the place, right De'Quan".

"Yes Mama".

"That's good. That's how I want yah to handle it, strictly a family thing. Quan always close the store with your mother", Pop said.

"Yes, of course Pop. I have Dre and Fat Pee on point too".

"Before I take this plea I'm going to see if I could get it lowered, but I doubt it. It's worth a try though".

The captain tapped on the window and signaled to Pop he had 5 minutes left. Pop shook his head then turned back to his family. "She's so fucking miserable".

They all laughed and Mama K said, "Okay, be nice yah. We're getting short on money too Pop".

"I know…I know that's why the store is so important. It will generate money while I'm up north".

De'Quan sat there thinking quietly to himself on how he could make things easier by giving Mama K his robbery money, without her asking him all types of questions. At the end of the day that's what the money was for anyway, so Mama K wouldn't have to stress for dough while Pop was locked away.

Suddenly keys jingled in the door and it swung open. They all stood up and Pop gave De'Quan a pound and a hug before he turned to Mama K. "I love you", they kissed in a warm embrace.

"Remember, yah always close the store with Mama K", Pop said staring into his son eyes before he was handcuffed and lead back through the big steel doors.

Chapter 12

Pop stalled the D.A.'s office for two months, but the offer stood. Either Pop was going to take the 7 ½ to 21years they were offering him or they were prepared to go trial. Pop said 'fuck it', took the time and the trip up north before things got out of hand with the court system.

De'Quan, Dre and Fat Pee did two more robberies within that two month time frame and things were beginning to look up for the young trio. De'Quan held strong on his thought's of Mama K going to need him to step up for the family while Pop was away, so he used Dre radiator to hold onto his stash of $1,300. Taking notes from Pop over the years De'Quan knew the key to a secure future was to keep stacking his dough.

Ne'Sean began to develop a love for playing basketball and it showed in the dedication he started putting into it with Jamel. They would go to the park everyday to play with the other kids in the projects to sharpen their skills. Word began to spread around Brooklyn Tech High School about Ne'Sean and Jamel being a good duo on the basketball court, prompting the junior varsity coach to put them on the team.

With one of her boys growing up faster than she can see and focus on, and her other son showing a new love for a gift they did not know he had when his father was home, Mama K was beginning to feel the pressure of having two boys in the house and no father around to keep them grounded. Everyday Mama K got the feeling of opening the store as an important piece to the entire family growth. No matter what state they were in Mama K knew she had to trust in Pop's plan, and stand by his side until he is able to come home and take them to the next level.

Mama K put $5,000 in Pop account when he was shipped upstate, so his commissary would be fat. Mama K had to laugh to herself, thinking Pop will try to figure out a way to flip that $5,000 while he's in there, instead of spending it on its intended purpose.

Things were pretty stable in Mama K's eyes, with a stash of $38,600 tucked in her mother house in Bushwick. She lined up a few vendors who were willing to supply her with the candy, food and drinks at a start up discount. The only delay was coming from the real estate company, who were shaky about leasing the store front to Grand-Ma Trina at such a late age. Making the acceptance of the check by the real estate company, the only thing left standing in Mama K's way.

Until one of life's curve balls was thrown her way.

Ring…Ring.

Grand-Ma Trina hustled from her stove over to the ringing telephone hanging on the wall. Grease popped out of the frying pan, as the rag she was using as pot holder brushed across one of the open flames, but she thought nothing of it as she dropped it on the counter and answered the phone, "Hello?"

"Hi Trina." It was her long time friend Ema.

"Oh…hey Ema. I was just thinking about you".

Grand-Ma Trina talked with her back turned to the counter, as the rag caught fire and the flames quickly jumped onto the kitchen window curtain. She smelled smoke, quickly turned around and panicked.

"Oh Lord!"

"What's going on?" Emma asked as the phone receiver left Grand-Ma Trina hand. The long slinky cord let the receiver hit the floor without bouncing back up into the air.

Grand-Ma Trina grabbed another rag, as the flames began to spread faster than she could move. She hit the flames with the rag, and her plan quickly began fail as that rag caught fire.

She blurted out another 'Oh Lord', and then she took off for the bathroom to get a bucket of water. Her dog Ginger began to bark historically from the back yard, repeatly scratching and ramming into the screen door. Smoke seeped out of the cracked kitchen window as the wall and ceiling started to catch fire.

Grand-Ma Trina ran back with a bucket of water and tripped on an old rip in the rug in the hallway. As she was falling, Trina cursed herself for promising to get that rip fixed and never doing it. She paid for it today by spilling the bucket all over the hallway rug instead of the fire on the other side of the wall.

'Oh please not my kitchen', was all that was going through Grand-Ma Trina mind as she scrabbled to her feet and ran back into the bathroom to refill the bucket. A loud crash almost made her heart stop as she hustled out of the bathroom to see what just happen.

Emma got scared when she heard Trina fall with the bucket of water. Emma quickly hung up the phone and dialed 911. When Emma finish explaining her story to the 911 operator, she hung up and quickly called Mama K before she put on her slippers and hurried herself over to Trina's house which was only two blocks away.

A police squad car cursing the area responded to the call. As the police pulled up in front of the house smoke began to float out of the living room window. Officer Benson hopped out of the curser and ran for the burning house, while his partner Officer Jimkoski radioed in for more help.

Officer Benson ran up against the locked door and began to pound on to see if he would get a response. When he didn't Officer Benson began to kick on the door until the locks gave way. He rushed pass a whiff of thick smoke, "it's the police, is anyone here?'

Grand-Ma Trina threw the second bucket of water into the kitchen from the doorway to avoid the thick smoke. "Yeah, I'm back here. Help me please".

Office Benson saw her through the smoke trying to feel her way back to the bathroom with a bucket in her hand. He quickly ran up on her and started pulling her down the hall.

"No...No. We have to save my kitchen!" Grand-Ma Trina protested as she tried to fight her way back into the thick smoke.

"Ma'am the fire department is on the way. Please let's go!"

Grand-Ma Trina began to cry as the smoke began to take a toll on her. Office Benson led her out of the burning house and into an EMS worker hands. As they put an oxygen mask on her face, Trina was able to blurt out Ginger's name.

"Who is that ma'am?" Officer Benson asked.

"My dog, she's in the backyard".

Officer Benson turned around and told the fire fighter's about the dog as they ran into the burning house.

Mama K had to park the car almost a block away from her mother house. Police officer's were pushing people away from the scene, as fire trucks and police cars clogged up the street. Mama K rushed over to the yellow tape barricade with Ne'Sean and Meika hot on her heels. Her mind was racing double time as she pushed her way through the light crowd.

"This is my mother's house!" Mama K barked when she was stopped at the barricade.

"Okay, let them through".

Mama K and the kids ran over to the EMS truck parked half way on the sidewalk, with its doors open. Grand-Ma Trina was crying with the oxygen mask on her face, as Emma held her hand and tried her best to console her friend.

"Ma what happen, you alright?" Mama K asked with confusion in her eyes. The kids ran over to their grandmother side as she sat on the back step of an ambulance. Tears streaming down her eyes as she breathed into an oxygen mask.

Grand- Ma Trina tried to speak but the oxygen mask made her words come out to distorted for Mama K patience. She turned to a fireman wearing a white helmet with a clip board in his hand and said, "Excuse me, can you please tell me what happen to my mother's house".

He stopped looking over his reports and said, "As far as we know the fire started in the kitchen".

"Where's Ginger? Her dog", Mama K asked.

"She's in the backyard, she's fine, just won't stop barking. The only way out of the backyard is through the house, and I'm not letting my men open that door. That dog is not a puppy and she's very upset. Once we get the house secured, you can go in and bring her out." The fire chief turned to Grand-Ma Trina and asked, "Ma'am can you tell me what happen?"

"I don't know! I turned around to answer the phone, and when I turned back around the curtains were on fire".

"You can go in and get the dog now. But you need a leash." One of the firemen said to Mama K. She reached in her purse and handed Ne'Sean ten dollars to go see if he could buy a leash in the corner store.

Grand-Ma Trina recapped her story and the fire chief said, "Well Ma'am, you're very lucky. I suggest you lock up the house and rest at your daughter house tonight. Give your house some time to air out. The back room upstairs is intact, but the kitchen ceiling fell down. So the bedroom still has a floor, but it's very unsafe to go in. You might want to call someone to check it out before you go in there.

"We believe the insulation that's placed in-between the ceiling and the upstairs floor caught fire, and it accelerated when some money caught fire in the same area. The money is burned up and unusable." His walkie-talkie started going off and he turned his back to answer it.

Grand-Ma Trina sat on the step of the EMS truck with a confused look on her face, "Money? What money?" She asked herself in a low tone.

In that moment, Mama K felt like she was just punched in her gut. Ne'Sean ran back to the truck with a leash he got the store owner to let him borrow and he pocketed the ten dollars his mother gave him. Two firemen escorted Mama K through house so she could get Ginger out of the back yard. She tried her best not to look through the ruins of her mother's house as thoughts of her real lost danced around in her mind.

Chapter 13

Once the area was cleared out, and the streets of Bushwick went back to normal, Mama K and Grand-Ma Trina went back into the house to grab some things, before they all piled into a cab and headed back to Marcy for the night.

De'Quan and Dre had been out all day planning their next hit and had no idea what was going on in his apartment. When they walked in it immediately felt like walking into a mad house. Meika and Ne'Sean were playing with Ginger in the living room with bags of clothes all over the place. Mama K, Grand-Ma Trina and Kim were in the kitchen making a big ruckus about getting Grand-Ma Trina house fixed, and De'Quan could swear he smelled smoke in the house.

"Where have you been?" Mama K snapped at him.

De'Quan just smoked a blunt of chocolate Ty from Marcy and Gates with Dre, making him slow on his feet. "We was…ah…we was on the other side. Why does it smell like fire in here?" De'Quan asked to shift the attention from him to something else.

"There was a fire in my house tonight," Grand-Ma Trina said with some sadness in her voice. She stood up and he gave her a hug.

"Wow Grand-Ma, what you going to do?" De'Quan asked.

Mama K spoke up, "they going to be staying with us for a while, you boys hungry?"

"Yes, but where yah going to sleep?"

Mama K snickered, "Don't worry your bunk bed is safe from Ginger. They sleeping in Meika room, and she will sleep with me. Tomorrow I want you to go with me and mommy over to her house so we can see what has to be done over there".

"Come on Dre, let's go in my room".

Mama K excused herself and went into the room behind them. She closed the door behind her and said, "I know you know everything Quan knows Dre, so both of you have a seat. I have to talk to yah".

"What's up Ma?"

She paced back and forth for a second, as De'Quan and Dre stared at her from the bottom bunk. Mama K took a deep breath and said, "The money is gone". Her voice almost broke down.

De'Quan and Dre snapped right out their high, as they both thought the same thing at the same time. 'How did they find the money in Dre's radiator?'

She continued before either of them could speak, "The fire started in Grand-Ma's kitchen, and it just so happens her bedroom is right on top of the kitchen. The whole damn ceiling fell on top of the fire and burned up the money Pop had in Grand-Ma floor".

Shaking her head, Mama K sat on the edge of the dresser craving a cigarette. Then she remembered she didn't smoke.

The boys breathed a sigh of relief that their little stash was still safe. "I didn't know Pop had money over there. I thought we were broke". De'Quan said feeling confused.

"Yeah well…It's gone now." She said clearly upset. "I needed that money to hold us down just in case the store plan didn't do too well".

"What you want to do now Mama K?" Dre asked.

She couldn't answer him.

De'Quan asked, "How much did you need for the store?"

"The down payment was 3,500.00, and that's already in the bank. The money in the floor was the just in case the store doesn't make enough money to cover or bills and inventory. Only until we did start to make a profit".

De'Quan looked over to Dre and they gave each other a slight nod. "By tomorrow we'll think of something Ma".

She nodded and said, "Yeah. By tomorrow, I'll have a plan together. I just wanted to let you know what's going on. Dre, you part of this family too. So it affects you too".

Her statement made Dre feel good inside to be recognized as a part of a more stable family.

She stood up and said, "Well you two go wash up and get ready to eat". Before she walked out of the room, Mama K took a look around like it this was the first time she walked into the boys room and said, "And clean up this damn room...place is a mess".

✳✳✳✳✳

Once Mama K was gone, De'Quan's mind went into over drive. "How much we got in the stash?"

"About 4,300, why, you want to give it to her?" Dre asked.

De'Quan jumped up and started pacing the room. "Shit! I got too. If I don't, this house will fall apart. We can hit that spot we scoped out, and we'll still be on top. That spot got at least five gees of better in it. We piece off Pee and we'll still have a little stash. What you think?"

Dre said, "I'm with you however you want to do it. But where we going to tell her we got the dough from?"

71

"Easy. We just say we spoke to G-Eyes that used to work for Pop, and we told him she was fucked up and we needed some work to get on, but instead of giving us drugs, he gave us the cash and we brought it straight to her. What you think?"

Frick and Frack is at work.

Dre said, "Yeah…that shit might work. It's hard as hell to find G-Eyes. She might not run into him for months".

"By then the store will already be jumping", De'Quan added with a smirk.

"Word". Dre said as they gave each other a pound.

"Let's go eat something. I got the munchies like a motherfucker".

Chapter 14

10:00a.m. the next morning Grand-Ma Trina, Mama K, De'Quan, and a neighborhood mister fix it name Mr. Jackson did a look over of the damaged house. Mama K felt a sharp pain in her stomach when they made their way into the kitchen. She had to remind herself to move on or fall apart. The money was gone.

De'Quan took one look at the inside of the kitchen and knew he was going to be out of $4,300 by the end of the night. Grand-Ma Trina had to hold onto Mama K's arm for strength as they made their way around the house.

Mr. Jackson went upstairs to assess the damage in the bedroom and came back down with the same warning the fire chief told them the night before. Upstairs would not be safe for Grand-Ma Trina to be in until they get the ceiling downstairs fixed first. After a long conversation it was established Mama K and Grand-Ma Trina would take care of the clean up. Once the ceiling was fixed, De'Quan and his friends will take care of the painting of the house to save them some money. It will take some time, but it was doable.

After a long day of skipping school and running with his mother De'Quan was ready for some action. He picked up Dre and they went downstairs to pull Fat Pee away from his cheeseburger and TV so they could handle their business. Their robbery G.A.M.E. (Ghetto's of America Misunderstanding on Escape) was starting to reach levels. They put some money together and purchased some new guns from Ju the gun seller from Dre side of the projects. They added a 16shot 9mm Taurus, a 15shot 9mm, and a 12 gage shotgun.

To make their getaways go by a little smoother Fat Pee learned how to steal cars, and in a short time, he became a good getaway driver, since his running skills were so suspect. Fat Pee kept the 12 gage in the car with him to give his partners great cover on the outside.

De'Quan and Dre had been watching a coke spot in Williamsburg for a couple of weeks and now the time was right to try their luck. To stack the $4,300 they had stashed, they had to rob too many stores. With each time feeling like it was getting harder and harder to get away. Robbing a drug spot would be more dangerous, but they all agreed the payout will be worth it. That's when De'Quan got wind of the under man spot in Williamsburg.

Fat Pee stole an Acura legend from Saratoga and Halsey, and they drove to Williamsburg in a nervous silence. No music, no smoking, and only thought's of surviving this next hit silently flowed through the car.

Fat Pee parked a block away from the private house and all three of them got out. They walked with a purpose through the shadows, unnoticed by anyone out on the cold winter night. After taking one last nervous look around De'Quan knocked on the door.

A sliding peephole slid open and a pair of eyes appeared, "What you want little nigga?"

"I work for Jah. He sent me to pick up for him", De'Quan said.

The peephole man thought for a second, and then said, "What Jah?'

"Tompkins Park Jah", De'Quan said with a slight attitude in his voice. If you act like you know what you talking about, you might catch him slipping. The slot was slammed and locks started clicking.

De'Quan stepped to the side making way for Fat Pee to lead the way with the shotgun. Fat Pee jammed it in the doorman face, "Don't even fart", he whispered, as Dre and De'Quan rushed pass them headed for the back room.

A brown skin man wearing a bent up New York Yankees hat sat behind an old card table counting money. He looked up in mid count and it took him too long to register what was about to happen him.

"Put your fucking hands up!" Dre screamed.

The man flinched in the direction of his gun that rested on his table filled with money, drugs and paraphernalia, but De'Quan was a step ahead of him. De'Quan knocked the gun on the floor with his left hand, and with gun wielding right hand he hit the man on the side of his head with the butt of his 9mm. The man fell out of his chair and crashed to the floor with a, "OWW...What the fuck man!"

"Shut the fuck up!" De'Quan said, as he stomped on the man's face, breaking his nose. Blood splattered all over the floor.

"Bring that other nigga in here", De'Quan yelled over his shoulder.

Fat Pee still had the shotgun in the doorman face as he led him to the back room, "Walk fucker".

De'Quan made the two dealers lay down on their stomachs, as Dre filled up his book bag with everything that was on top of the card table. De'Quan patted the two men down taking their money, keys and any loose change they had in their pockets, "take that jewelry off...and those shoes too".

"What the fuck you want their nasty ass shoes for?" Fat Pee asked shocked De'Quan was into taking dudes shoes now.

"So they can't follow us", Dre answered.

That's when a light went off in De'Quan's head, "Yo F.P. go start the car".

"Why the fuck did you just say my name?" Fat Pee said, fuming.

De'Quan snapped back at him, "Man, just do what I said. We right behind you".

Dre knew something was up. Fat Pee looked around the quiet room, sucked his teeth, and then ran out the door to go start the car. Dre put the heavy book bag on his back and asked, "What's up?"

De'Quan picked up the dealer's gun, "We do them with their own guns, and throw these shits off the Brooklyn Bridge. What up, you down?"

Dre searched De'Quan's face for a trace of a smile. He couldn't find one. De'Quan was dead serious.

"I'm…I'm saying…It's on you", Dre said. He tried to swallow after saying it, but his throat was drier than Arizona.

To make sure Dre was down, De'Quan said, "I hit one. You hit one."

Before Dre could answer him, De'Quan stepped up and shot the doorman point blank in the back of his head. Everybody in the room jumped at the loud sound of the dealer gun. The table man began to plead his case from the floor.

"Hey listen young blood, I didn't see-"

"Shut the fuck up!" De'Quan barked, as he handed the gun to Dre.

"Hey listen, just let me go and I'll forget your faces and this whole shit. I'll even get rid of Ol Tuffy over here."

"Man if I to tell you again. Dre shoot this fagget!"

The man began to piss on himself. "Aww come on little man, you do have to do this," He cried.

"Dre, the nigga saw our faces. They will come to the projects and kill us. So shoot this nigga and let's go."

Dre began to sweat like he just took a shower with his clothes on. His hands were so clammy, Dre just wanted to let the gun slip out of his hand and he run up out of there.

"Let's Go! Shoot him Dre!"

Dre pulled the trigger three times silencing the whining table man. The action brought a smile to De'Quan's face. No matter what Dre will always be his brother. "Come on!"

They ran out of the house and hopped into the waiting car. Dre laid down on the backseat floor as Fat Pee pilled off into traffic. Fat Pee dropped them off at Dre's building, and then drove to Queens to drop off the stolen car.

It was 11:10p.m and all was quiet in Dre apartment. His sister was in her room asleep, and Dre mother wasn't home. De'Quan sat on Dre bed and began to roll a blunt, as Dre paced the room. They were waiting for Fat Pee to return before they counted up their booty.

Dre tried to keep his voice as low as possible, "Damn Quan, I didn't' know we were going to kill them dudes."

De'Quan tried to look cool as fan when he looked up from the blunt he was rolling and said, "Just chill Dre, them dudes were some serious dudes who saw our faces. When I thought about it, I said 'shit what would I do if I was them?

"Then it hit me, find out where they from and go kill their asses. They saw our faces and we couldn't get in there wearing masks. Give me a light, shit got my nerves all fucked up."

Dre grabbed the lighter off the dresser and handed it to him, "I guess you right. Shit just caught me off guard."

"You think that caught you off guard, wait till you smoke some of this chocolate ty."

By the time Fat Pee got back from dumping the car Dre and De'Quan were sitting in a chocolate ty stupor. Fat Pee grabbed the crate to sit on and said, "Yo what happen in there? I thought I heard shots when I was starting the car."

Dre and De'Quan just stared at him. Then they looked at each other and burst out laughing.

"What the fuck is so funny?" Fat Pee snapped.

"Man you sounded like you was about to cry just now," Dre said still chuckling.

Fat Pee looked around the room with a stupid look on his face making them laugh at him harder. "Matter of fact, where the weed at, niggas ain't going to be laughing at me all night."

De'Quan gave Fat Pee what was left of the blunt and said, "Nah, but on some real shit, we had to smoke them dudes."

Fat Pee took a long pull of the blunt and almost chocked, "What…what the fuck for?"

Dre said, "Because they saw our faces Pee, and they would have come looking for us. That's how big time dudes get down son."

De'Quan jumped in, "Yeah Pee…and when you left the boss nigga asked who we said we came for again. That alone tells you they would have come looking for us."

Dre continued the double team, "The last thing we need is for some big time dudes to come through the projects looking for us. And what's up with you acting like there's some love lost for them niggas?" Dre said flipping it on Fat Pee.

"Naw man", Fat Pee took a strong pull from the blunt clip and said, "It was on my mind that I thought I heard shots, and maybe they tried to move on yah when I left. That's all. I really don't care what happen to them, as long as we got away and we get to count this dough."

"Yeah, that's what I'm talking about", De'Quan said with a big smile. "Counting that dough." He grabbed the bag and dumped it's contains out on the floor. Dre pushed the dresser onto the door and they all just stared at all the money and drugs on the floor.

Dre broke the silence, "Damn! I ain't never seen so much dough before in my life."

"Word! We are fucking rich now dawg", Fat Pee said with a big kool-aid smile on his face. Dre and De'Quan started laughing and they all dug into stacks of cash and started separating it.

When they were finished, they were staring at $35,753 in cash, and $11,240 worth of cocaine. Everyone was lost in his own thoughts for a minute until De'Quan finally broke the silence, "Ok, this is how we freak this. We do our usual split of the dough, but the drugs, I say we flush it."

Dre snapped out of his high real quick, "What? Why the fuck would we do that?"

"For one we ain't no drug dealers, and for two how we going to look coming out of nowhere with 11 thousand dollars worth of drugs to sell all of a sudden. Shit and where would we sell it at if we could?" De'Quan said in Dre's direction. De'Quan knew Fat Pee will go with any plan that sounds good to him and Dre.

Dre said, "Naw man, I say we sit on it for a rainy day. What if we go out, and get crazy and spend all of our dough, we going to be fucked up if we can't find another spot to rob, but if we have this coke to fall back on we good for a minute."

Fat Pee added his two cents, "Now that sounds like a plan instead of flushing it down the toilet."

De'Quan scratched his head, "Alright, it makes sense. We sit on it then. Pop taught me a long time ago coke won't go bad as long as we keep it cool."

They did their split of the money and when they were finish, Fat Pee looked like he was ready to run out the door. Dre eyed him hard, "Pee why don't you leave some of that in the window stash".

Fat Pee blinked, and got on the defensive, "For what".

De'Quan approached him from another angle, "Pee we know about you and Sugar. The streets are talking".

Fat Pee looked like he just got caught stealing out of the candy jar. "Yeah, so what. I don't care about what the streets is saying".

"Yo keep your voice down before you wake up Shakia", Dre snapped. "Anyway, it's your money and you can spend it on anything you want, but 12gees is a lot of dough Pee. The last thing we need is for Sugar – or anybody else for that matter – to be questioning where we get dough from, you feel me".

Fat Pee remained on the defensive, "Fuck I look like telling some chick our business?" He stood up and started stuffing money in his pockets. "Yah acting like a nigga pussy whipped or something".

De'Quan stood up to face him, "Nah Pee it ain't like that. We just saying now we playing with some real money, and we don't need anybody asking us shit about shit".

Fat Pee sat back down on the crate and lit up a cigarette, "Yeah yah said that already".

De'Quan put his hand on his shoulder and said, "Pee, we brothers man, and we're only watching each other's back".

Dre jumped in, "Yeah, that's all I'm saying Pee. So if you want to leave some here, you'll be alright is all I'm saying".

Fat Pee sat there thinking about it as De'Quan put a new agenda on the table, "Before I forget, we have to buy some new guns too. Dre make it happen with Ju and see if we can get some new nines for a good price. We all can put a gee to the side for that".

They each counted out a thousand dollars and Dre rubber band it together. De'Quan took the $4,300 out of the stash, then he and Dre put ten thousand each of the their money back in the stash spot. Fat Pee watched all of this and thought to himself 'fuck it'.

Fat Pee counted out five thousand and said, "Here, put this in there".

"When we going to dump these dirty guns?" Dre asked.

"Tomorrow, so get on Ju", De'Quan said.

"We should get some big joint's from him", Fat Pee suggested.

"We will", De'Quan stuffed the $4,300 in his pocket, and his $1,000 of spending money in his other pocket. "What you going to do with all that dough Quan?" Fat Pee asked.

"Mama K is fucked up right now. My Grand-Mom's crib caught fire the other day and Pops money burned up in there. So I'm blessing her with this so she can still open up the store".

"Word, damn", Fat Pee said.

De'Quan put on his jacket and said, "I'm tired. Come on Pee, let's bounce".

"Word. I'm mad hungry too".

Dre walked them to the door and said, "Don't eat five gees worth of White Castles in one night".

They all laughed, "Whatever man. Later". They gave Dre a pound, and then headed down the stairs.

*****

De'Quan crept into the house and was surprised to run into Mama K sitting at the kitchen table nursing a cigarette, something he never saw her do. He locked the door and went into the kitchen to sit with her.

"I thought you would spend the night at Dre's house tonight when I didn't see you at 11". Mama K said, surprised he was coming in so late.

"Sorry Ma. We was chilling and I lost track of time", De'Quan said.

Mama K put the cigarette out as De'Quan dug into his pocket and pulled out the money. He slowly put it on the table and Mama K's eyes grew wide under the dim kitchen light.

"Where did you get that?"

De'Quan shifted in his seat and said, "Me and Dre went to see G-Eyes".

"I know yah ain't been out here selling drugs, after I told you not too", Mama K said trying her best not to raise her voice.

De'Quan put on his performance face and said, "No Mama. I'm not going to lie, we went to him to get something from him, but he gave us the cash instead. I know what you told us, but we can't just sit back and watch you struggle on your own all the time. The store is important to you and Pop and we was just trying to help, if we could".

She slowly took the money and began to count it. As Mama K counted her anger began to subside and was replaced with amazement, "4,300, wow Quan, I needed this. Tell him thank you", she said reaching across the table to take his hand.

"You know I love you, and I don't want you boys out there doing no crazy things. I can't lose yah to these streets. I already lost Pop, and losing yah will break my heart even more".

"Don't worry Mama, we'll be here", De'Quan said with a tired smile.

She stood up and gave him a hug, "Thank you baby. Now go get some rest. I'll see you in the morning".

Chapter 15

"Welcome To The Rucker New York City! The junior tournament is in full effect today!" The crowd roared with approval over the background music in New York City's infamous Rucker Park. The screaming crowd stretched from the bleachers out onto the street. Heads hung out the windows of the school, and surrounding buildings shouting out their hood, but were out done by the spectators who let their presence from the roof tops be heard in the famous park.

"In the red jerseys we got the visitors representing Brook-nom! Let me hear it for the Bed-Stuy Heat!"The M.C.

said igniting a loud chant of 'Brooook-lyn!' from the hot summer time crowd.

"And in the black with white trim we got The Squad-representing The B.X. baby! Uptown give it up!" The crowd screamed even louder for its uptown favorite.

"Okay, yah know the rules…let your game do the talking and the losers do the walking!" the M.C. had the crowd in a frenzy, as LL cool J told all the girl's out of the park speakers how they were 'Jiggling Baby'. The bleachers was packed with a mixture of New York City's elite, basketball fanatics, high class honey's, baller's, and kids just out to have a good time.

8th Avenue was like a ghetto car show. Whips were freshly waxed as heads from up and down the east coast flocked to New York City traditional basketball tournament, where stars where made and bums was sent home with a broken heart. The atmosphere at the Rucker is always live and full of energy.

De'Quan, Dre, Fat Pee, and Rahkem sat in the bleachers absorbing the whole Rucker high as they watched Ne'Sean and his team the Bed-Stuy Heat represent on the New York stage. De'Quan also had in mind to scope out some of the big time dealers who felt the need to pull out their most expensive car, and shiniest jewelry for this festive event. They needed a new vic and what better place to find one on a hot Saturday afternoon.

"Now this is it yah. Let's bring it back to Brooklyn!" The coach barked from the middle of the huddle.

"Yeah, that's what I'm talking about!" Their center Lay Lay yelled in the huddle. He stood at 6'4 and was lanky, but what he lacked in size he made up with speed and skill on the court. "B.K. on three…1-2-3!"

"B.K." and the starting five took the court. Ne'Sean was big enough to be the team starting forward. Jamel was the point guard, Lay Lay at center, Taz at power forward, and Bliz at shooting guard. They jumped right into their business by winning the opening tip and scoring the first two points of the game.

De'Quan was into the game, while Dre sat back and analyzed the action that was popping on 8th Avenue. Dre focused on a dark skin brother with a fade, sporting a pair of Gucci shades. He was dipped out in a grey Nike suit with the uptowns to match. He was all smiles as he sat on the hood of a blue 325i BMW, with two summer bunnies standing in front of him, ke-keing at his every joke.

Dre nudged De'Quan in his side, "You see son sitting over there on that blue three and a quarter?"

De'Quan took his eyes off the game for a moment and scanned the action on 8th Avenue, "Yeah I see him. What about him?"

"You don't recognize duke?"

De'Quan was on the verge of being aggravated. Dre was disturbing his game watching. "No Dre, I don't know that dude, now what."

"That's that dude Shaborn from that hood in Queens...Lefrak", Dre said.

De'Quan stared at Dre with a lost look in his eyes, so Dre pressed on, "The dude from that club we were at, when those bitches were running their mouths about how son paper is long and how he got a section in Lefrak on lock. You don't remember that?"

De'Quan looked back over in Shaborn's direction with a different focus in his eyes. "Ohh yeah...I remember who son is now, but we don't know shit about him".

"Nah we don't, but peep the chick on his left hand side", Dre said with a smirk on his face.

De'Quan looked over at the girl and he wasn't sure about who he thought he was looking at, "Damn, she looks like Tasha from here".

"That's who that is my man", Dre said grinning. "I see it like this, we keep an eye on her ass, cause Tasha always gets her man. We follow her to duke, and Bam we got an easy, but official vic. What you think?"

De'Quan's mind started clicking with his partner until a smile finally crept on his face. The crowd around them erupted forcing them to turn to the basketball court. Fat Pee and Rahkem were losing all of their cool point's as they jumped up and high fived each other, Oh Shit! You saw what Sean just did to son ankles?"

"Word", Rahkem said giving Fat Pee another pound.

"My brother is going to the NBA one day", De'Quan said only loud enough for Dre to hear him.

Dre shook his head in agreement, "Yeah I can see it. He got mad ups now, so imagine in...Oh Shit!"

Ne'Sean shook the kid guarding him and threw an ally-op to Taz, who finished off the play with a monster slam sending the park over the top as it exploded into another round of cheers and chants of 'Brooook-lyn'.

*****

"Mama! Mama where you at?" Ne'Sean loudly called down the apartment hallway. His loud entourage rolled in behind him and flooded the living room with replays of the game still fresh on their minds.

"What happen?" Mama K asked as she shuffled down the hallway with Grand-Ma Trina hot on her heels.

Ne'Sean wore a big smile as he held up his trophy he won with the Bed-Stuy Heat at the Rucker.

"Oh my goodness, yah won", Mama K said giving him a big hug. "I'm proud of you baby".

"He put on a show out there today Mama K, but now we have to change and go to the victory party", De'Quan said.

"Well not before I get my hugs and kisses", Grand-Ma Trina said coming down the hallway. "I'm proud of you too baby", she said as she pushed Mama K and De'Quan to the side to get to Ne'Sean sparking a round of laughs throughout the house.

The victory party was held in building 520 in Marcy. No one cared whose apartment it was, all they cared about was Brooklyn beat the Bronx at the Rucker and brought the trophy home. E.P.M.D. was giving everybody the business out of a set of large speakers that could be heard throughout the building. The atmosphere was soaked with weed smoke, laughter, and game being shot by both sexes in all directions.

De'Quan sported his brother to all of the girls in the party until he set his eyes on a coco brown cutie. She was dipped out in a sandy brown D.K.N.Y. velour suit, as she held up a back wall. She whispered something to her friend at her side and when she turned back around, she locked eyes with De'Quan.

De'Quan stepped to them with Ne'Sean at his side, "Excuse me ladies. I don't mean to disturb your conversation or anything. I just wanted to introduce yah to my brother Ne'Sean. The star of the Rucker show today".

Coco brown had been eyeing De'Quan all night and she was wondering when he was going to notice her. She had butterflies in her stomach when she said, "Yeah we heard. Sorry we missed your game".

De'Quan lightly pushed Ne'Sean in the small of his back toward her friend, "What's your name pretty?" Ne'Sean asked the friend.

A big smile crawled into the corners of her mouth, "Janet and this is my friend Mecca".

Ne'Sean looked over to Mecca and said, "Hi, can I borrow your friend for the dance floor?"

Mecca giggled, "As long as you not trying to steal her away from me. I know your brother can keep me company until yah come back".

They all chuckled and Janet said, "Girl, I hope we both get stolen".

The two girls snicker as De'Quan whispered into Ne'Sean's ear, "We definitely fucking tonight". The brothers laughed then partied the night away with their two new friends.

Chapter 16

Two days after the party, Dre sat on the back of the park bench waiting for De'Quan to come downstairs. It was almost noon and it was already a scorching summer day out front of De'Quan's building with the usual activity of crack heads coming and going at a steady pace. Dre paid all this activity little mind because it had nothing to do with him, until the chaos unfolded before his very eyes.

"T-N-T...T-N-T! Don't move motherfucker!"

"Freeze!"

40 ounces dropped, crack heads were quickly tackled as they cried their innocence, and two T-N-T officers got into a fist fight with one of the dealers in De'Quan's lobby. Dre quickly snapped out of his trance and tried to make his way off of the bench to head in the opposite direction.

"Don't fucking move asshole! Get on the ground! Get on the ground!"

Dre turned to the screaming voice and he was surprised to come face to face with the nozzle of a 38 special. Dre was knocked off of his feet by the 250 pound officer and slammed down to the ground. The officer speed searched Dre with his free hand as he kept his gun aimed at Dre's head.

When he reached Dre's waist band he pulled out a 9mm browning pistol, "I got one! I got one!" The officer called out over his shoulder. He threw Dre's gun to the side, holstered his gun and hand cuffed Dre.

De'Quan was coming down the stairs when he heard scuffling going on in the lobby. He thought it was the usual scene of a dealer beating up a crack head for being short on the money, until he heard the squawk of a walkie-talkie goes off. De'Quan did a 180 and ran back upstairs to his house.

When he ran inside De'Quan ran straight for the window. When he looked to the right of the benches, he saw a big white cop lift Dre off of the ground as if he only weighed only 20 pounds.

"Mama K! Mama K! Come quick", De'Quan called out over his shoulder as he kept his eyes on the scene playing out in front of his building.

Mama K shuffled down the hallway and over to the window, "What's wrong?" She asked, than took a look out the window before he could answer her. Mama K came just in time to see the officer hit Dre in his head with the walkie-talkie, as he was stuffing Dre in the back of a caravan.

Mama K turned from the window without saying a word and ran out the door. She ran down the steps two at a time and came out the front of the building like a young sister ready for an after school fight.

"What hell are yah doing to my son?" Mama K said as she stepped to the small crowd by the caravan. "What's going on here?"

"Who's your son ma'am?" A Latino officer asked as his directed the scene.

Mama K looked through the tinted windows of the caravan and pointed to Dre, "Him".

She made a move to open the door and the Latino officer stepped in between her and the door, "Hold on ma'am, if you talking about little Billy the kid back there, we just found a 9mm on him, so he's going to see the judge about that".

Mama K blinked and said, "A gun". She quickly thought about what she walked into and knew there was no way she was going to get Dre out the back of that caravan.

"Yes ma'am a gun. Now what is his name?" The officer asked her thinking she was ready to talk to him.

Mama K looked him up and down and said, "Ask him", and with that she turned on her heels and headed back to the building. When she got back into the house De'Quan was all over the place, "Mama K we have to get him out. Damn!"

"Quan calm down. We're going to get him out. We have to wait for him to see the judge first, which will probably be in two days".

"Two Days!"

"Boy, stop yelling up in this house. Now go sit down somewhere, while I go call his mother and see if she can get some bail money together". As soon as she said it, she wanted to take it back. Everyone knew Dre's mother drinks her money away and she didn't have any friends who were worth more than wine money.

De'Quan sucked his teeth and said, "I'll get the money".

"Now don't you go out there and do something stupid. It's bad enough yah running around here with guns and shit". She cursed some more under her breath and walked into the kitchen to use the phone.

De'Quan did not want to tell her they had money stashed in Dre's room. He just stood there quiet thinking about how he was going to get into Dre's room. He got an idea and slipped out of the house while Mama K was still on the phone.

$$\ast\ast\ast\ast\ast$$

Fat Pee was on the Flushing side of the projects trying to get in a good sweat on the basketball court when De'Quan found him. De'Quan stepped right onto the court, "Yo Pee, come here for a minute".

Fat Pee looked over and saw De'Quan walking on to the court with a purpose, "What's up. This game is almost-"

De'Quan cut him off, "Nah, we got to talk right now".

Fat Pee saw the seriousness in his friend eyes and he knew his game was over, "Yo Jah, take my place son". Fat Pee walked off of the court with De'Quan and as soon as they were out of ear shot Fat Pee asked him, "What's up Quan?"

"Dre got knocked like 20 minutes ago in front of my building by T-N-T".

"What do you mean T-N-T? Dre don't sell no drugs", Fat Pee said with a lost look in his eyes.

De'Quan filled him in on what happened to Dre in front of his building. "Look we have to bail him out. The problem is our money is in his house. We can't let his moms know about the stash, she will dead us on the rest and drink it away. His sister I'm not too sure about. Damn, I never thought this shit would happen".

Fat Pee grabbed his pants off of the bench and started getting dressed. De'Quan hopped on the bench and fished out a cigarette. Just when he put a flame to his cigarette, an argument broke out over the basketball game.

A little skin pretty boy type started arguing with a tall brown skin brother over a foul. The pretty boy walked over to another section of benches and said something to a girl that sitting by herself.

"Check the ball then nigga!" The pretty boy said as he walked back onto the court.

90

The brown skin brother through the ball at him faster than the pretty boy could react, and the ball slipped through his fingers and popped him in his chest.

Pretty boy lost his cool, "Toi, give me that!"

The girl quickly hopped off of the bench and ran toward him like a cornered cat. He snatched the coach bag out of her hands and pulled out a 9mm berretta. Chaos engulfed the parkas the automatic barked across the afternoon sky.

Pop, Pop, Pop.

"Yeah you bitch ass nigga. What's up now?" The pretty boy yelled as everybody scattered, ducking for cover.

Fat Pee had on his pants, but his sneakers were still untied. When the shooting started Fat Pee followed De'Quan to the nearest park exit, but 10 feet from the gate, he tripped on his laces and fell face first on the black top.

De'Quan felt something wasn't right behind him and turned just in time to see Fat Pee getting up in a cross fire. De'Quan pulled out his 45 and let off two rounds in pretty boy direction. "Come on Pee, I got you".

"Oh you want some of this too?" Pretty boy barked as he aimed his gun at De'Quan.

Fat Pee got behind his friend as De'Quan stood his ground, "Nah son, we just going to go about our business. That's it". De'Quan and Fat Pee began to back their way out of the park.

Toi snapped her man out of his trance, "Pooh the police is coming!"

Pooh turned from his stare down with De'Quan, "Oh shit, let's go", Pooh said and ran for another hole in the park fence with Toi hot on his heels.

Fat Pee and De'Quan made it to Fat Pee's house and walked into another chaotic scene. Fat Pee mother stomped through the house beefing about something, while his two younger siblings tore up the livingroom like they were playing in the sand park. Fat Pee ignored the drama and walked straight to his room with De'Quan following him in a daze. The whole projects had gone mad.

De'Quan sat on Fat Pee bed and said, "This day is getting crazier by the minute. Yo what the fuck is going on in your livingroom dawg?"

Fat Pee peeled out of his shirt and said, "Who cares. Yo that nigga was talking shit all game".

De'Quan said, "Fuck that nigga. Anyway, like I was telling you we have to get Dre up out of there. You got any 45 bullets in here?"

Fat Pee open up his closet reviling close to 30 boxes of sneakers, and did a quick scan. When he saw the box he wanted, Fat Pee pulled it out and took it over to the bed. Inside the Nike box, he had a stack of money, two guns, and over fifty loose bullets. He took the money out and let De'Quan fish through the sea of bullets for what he needed.

When Fat Pee finished counting the money he said, "I got a little over thirty five hundred. If we need more than that, then I guess one of us is going to have to promise Dre's sister a good time, in exchange to let us in his room for a minute".

De'Quan busted out laughing, took the clip out of his gun and replaced the two shells he let off in the park. "That should be enough. Man we got to start spreading this money out. We can't have this shit happen again. You got some weed?"

"Yeah. Yo where we go to pay his bail?" Fat Pee asked as he searched his secret stashes for his weed and Phillies.

I don't know. Mama K knows all that stuff. When I left her, she was on the phone calling about that stuff. We go see what she talking about after this blunt. I got to relax for a minute".

Fat pee chuckled and said, "We all do bro. These streets are crazy".

De'Quan laughed, "Nigga your crib is crazy".

Fat Pee laughed harder, "I know".

Chapter 17

Central Bookings in downtown Brooklyn is where Dre found himself roasting in a hot holding cell. Disgusted that he got caught slipping like that. He was currently sharing a cell with a dope fiend who must have the nodding record. Dre watched the dope fiend sit on the bench across from him and nod forward, with a long glob of spit hanging out the corner of his mouth, for four hours straight. Dre couldn't believe it.

Dre had been sitting in the same nasty cell for thirty hours and this stomach was doing back flips, because he hadn't eaten since he left his house. The police tried to feed Dre a baloney and cheese sandwich that looked half brown. Dre gave his away.

War stories were being told by other prisoners every hour on the hour like 10-10 wins, and Dre was tired of listening to it. He tried getting sleep, but every time he heard keys rattling, he would snap to attention in hopes of moving on to see the judge. Thought's of having to use the bathroom kept invading Dre's mind, but one look at the toilet stopped him from taking a piss half the time.

"Alright, listen up!" The chatter floating down the small cell block quickly faded. "When I call your name, step up and step out. You will be cuffed, put on a bus and taken to court this morning. First man, Willie Johnson, Andre Jones, Michael Black".

Dre didn't care what the c.o. said after he called his name, as long as he called it. At Brooklyn criminal court house Dre was put in another holding cell for five more hours before he was put on a six man chain gang and brought upstairs on an elevator to the second floor.

Dre and the rest of the chain gang were put into a much cleaner cell, and more action was taking place with lawyers pay guys visits.

"Andre Jones!"

"Yeah! Right here!" Dre made his way to the front of the cell. He was relieved to come face to face with a black man with a salt and pepper mini-afro. He was dressed in a brown suit and he looked like he hadn't shaved in three weeks.

"I'm Mr. Gordon Winston, here take my card", he said in a Caribbean accent. "Now Andre this is your first offense, so we might be able to get you an R.O.R. with no problem. Your mother and brother are out there", he said looking down at some papers. "Mama K and huh, De'Quan. They said they have bail money. I told them I might be able to get the R.O.R. So I'll see you out there", Mr. Winston said and quickly ran off as quick as he came. Dre didn't get two words in, just a bunch of head nods.

Ten minutes later Dre's name was called again and this time he was pushed out into the courtroom like he was being fed to the wolves. He walked over to the table he saw Mr. Winston standing at and stared down at the bright yellow arrow that was taped to the table that said 'You stand here' in bright red letters.

Dre did a quick turn around and scanned the faces in the crowd courtroom. He saw Mama K, De'Quan and Fat Pee sitting in the mist of the tired faces in the back. He felt a good feeling inside when they locked eyes.

Mr. Winston and the assistant district attorney went back and forth in a language of legalized bullshit Dre didn't understand until the judge said, "R.O.R. Clerk issue the defendant a return date and a slip please, next".

Dre quickly took his pink slip and made his exit through the plastic chain link barrier. He gave Mama K a hug, and gave De'Quan and Fat Pee a pound, as Mama K thanked Mr. Winston.

They headed out of the court building and walked to Mama K's car, but not without the sermon they all knew was coming. "I hope this is the last trip I'm gonna have to make to this court for one of you boys. Because I'm telling you now, yah better start being more careful out in these streets. Start thinking about what yah want to do with your lives".

The boys remained silent as the piled into the car and Mama K continued, "You boys are a month and some change out of high school and don't know what yah want to do. Well I'm going to tell you like this, yah better straighten up, and think about getting some jobs or come work with me in the store. I'm not going to lose one of you to these streets. Dre and Paul, you too are like one of my own and yah know this. Boys I love all three of yah and I don't want nothing happening to yah. You understand".

They all replied with low murmured 'yes's' and fell back into quiet mode. Mama pulled over the car in front of Dre's building and all three of the boys jumped out. Dre hesitated before he said, "Mama K why my mother didn't come?"

Mama K anticipated Dre asking this question, "I spoke with her and she was out trying to get some bail money, just in case we needed it. But we didn't, so everything is okay, right", she said, putting on a smile to relax Dre mind. Truth was Dre's mother was too drunk to go with them to the court house. Mama K knew it was best to keep that to herself.

Dre smiled, "Thanks Mama K". He leaned into the driver's side window and gave her a kiss on her cheek.

"Don't worry about it baby. You boys be careful and think about what I said about doing something with your lives". They all nodded as she pulled off from the curb.

*****

Dre tried to get his thoughts together in the shower, while Fat Pee and De'Quan played street fighter on his super Nintendo in the mist of large clouds of smoke. Spending thirty plus hours in the slammer gave Dre a lot to think about and it was time they stepped their game up. Mama K was right in her own little way. They definitely couldn't go on like this forever. They needed a real plan. They were some real niggas, and the way Dre saw it Real Always Wins in the end. A major plan was a definite must.

Dre dried off, wrapped the towel around himself, and shaved the little bit of facial hair he had. After brushing his teeth, putting on lotion, a white T, and a crisp pair of boxers Dre felt like a new man. Staring at himself in the mirror Dre felt a light surge of energy. "Yeah, I'm ready", He said to himself with a big smile.

Dre walked into his room into a loud cloud of smoke, and an atmosphere of cursing and kung-fu noise from the TV.

"Just what I needed," Dre said.

Fat Pee smirked and said, "What nigga, a shower?"

De'Quan started laughing. Dre said, "No nigga, this blunt", and with that, Dre snatched the blunt out of Fat Pee hand.

De'Quan laughed harder. His two friends always went at it for the entertainment in it, but if an outsider ever made the mistake of taking their cracks on each other as a weakness for their love for each other, they would pay for their mistake. De'Quan said, "What up Dre, did anybody try you for your kicks up in there?"

Dre blew out a deep cloud of smoke and said, "Hell no. Marcy is running shit up in there".

"Yeah, that's what I'm talking about. Pop didn't have any problems on the Island, and he was shot the fuck up. And niggas recognize Pop up north", De'Quan said with some pride.

Fat Pee jumped in, "That's word. Pop up in Clinton with my uncle Tech, from building 621. Tech said 'they living it up B.K. style".

De'Quan put down his joy stick and said, "So, what's next yah? We got to make a hit, and we have to change this situation with the stash spot. Dre, we was fucked up if your bail was more than five gees. I didn't know how we were going to get up in this house".

"I think we should put our bread in four different places", Dre said, sharing one of his thought's he brain stormed in the cell. "I did wonder how yah were going to get in here to get the money".

Fat Pee said, "four places, where we going to find four places' at?'

De'Quan said, "Well we can use our three houses, and we need one good stash spot we all have access to".

"What about a chick crib?" fat Pee said.

Dre said, "Hell no! I'm not trusting no female with my money, unless it's Mama K or my sister".

De'Quan said, "I can go for that. Mama K is the only female I would trust with my money too, but we can't go that route, so what's next?"

"I got it. We can make Rah the holder. Like our treasurer or some shit", Dre said.

"Now I can go for that. We put it to him like this; he holds the sneaker box for us. It will only have money in it, and if anything comes up missing, it's on him. We can't lose. Rah is scared of us, he'll jump out the window, before he spends some of our dough", Fat Pee said.

De'Quan agreed, "Word, that's a good idea. If any one of us gets in a situation like Dre did, then the rest of us still has access to the money to take care of bail and other things".

Dre started getting dress, "So we knick out the four places and just focus on one".

De'Quan said, "Yeah, I mean Rah's crib can be our major stash spot, and of course we all will have some dough in our own cribs like Pee did. Pee had a stash, and I had a gee to put with it for your bail".

Fat Pee said, "Yeah nigga, don't you forget who was coming to get your ass".

"Shut the fuck up. You know you my son. You better had came to get par-par out, or I would have put my foot in your ass", Dre said sparking a round of laughs around the room.

De'Quan calmed down and said, "what was you going to tell me before you got knocked?"

Dre looked at him with a lost look in his eyes, than it hit him, "Oh yeah. Remember the dude Shaborn from Lefrek we were watching at the Rucker?"

"The dude Tasha was all over, yeah I remember. What about him?" De'Quan asked.

Dre said, "Dig it, I ran up on her the other day on some trying to get some pussy shit right. She starts acting all high sadiddy and shit, so I took a stab in the dark and said, 'why, cause you fucking wit that nigga Sha?' and her whole face changed. She asked me how I know, but I side stepped the question with a, who doesn't know your business answer. Then I stepped off.

"Later on I followed her to Queens and she took me right to his spot. He's in a three family house, in the back streets of Lefrek city. Shaborn lives on the third floor, and there's a family living on the ground floor. The middle floor is empty", Dre said.

De'Quan's mind started turning. He was the one who always figured out how they got in and out of a place. "Do you think they will hear us kick in the door?"

"Hell yeah, the wall are super thin in a house like that", Dre said.

Fat Pee interjected, "Why don't we just stake it out, and see how we get in that way".

Dre said, "word, we can do that".

De'Quan said, "Aight, fuck it. We take shifts on him. This could be the big one, so we have to plan this one out to the tee. No fuck ups".

Chapter 18

Mama K was digging her new home away from home. With Pop making some calls from behind the wall, the paperwork finally cleared and Mama K was able to open up the first legal family business. Mama K had a nice little grand opening at her new store on Lewis Avenue and Green Street. Even though a few people wandered into the store thinking she was opening up a new weed spot in the hood, Mama K was still enjoying herself and the new people she was meeting every day.

Most of Meika's day consisted of her and her friends hanging around the store for the air conditioning, and to give Mama K a helping hand around the store. De'Quan helped out on the close up like he said he would, while Ne'Sean tried his best to stay away from the store, unless he wanted something.

It was another hot summer day in Brooklyn and the action walking pass the store is what had De'Quan and Dre attention, as they sat on milk creates, sipping on juices. The two friends had been enjoying their pick of the many flavors of ladies that strolled by all day.

Dre eyed a brown skin cutie coming down the block in a yellow sundress, "I got this one", he said quickly staking his claim.

De'Quan shrugged her off, "Play on player".

"Quan, the phone!" Meika yelled from the back of the store.

"A'ight", he answered and got off his create. "Dre, don't hurt yourself out here".

"I hear you", Dre shot back as he watched sundress make her way closer to the store. When she got close enough Dre said, "Excuse me".

She stopped in her tracks and looked down at him. When it was obvious he wasn't getting up from his seat, she almost walked off. Dre reached out as he stood and said, "Hey, hold on a second. My name is Dre and I won't keep you long. Unless you in a rush".

With a straight face she said, "I might be, it all depends".

Dre thought to himself 'I got her'.

De'Quan picked up the hanging receiver, "Hello".

"Yo what's up?" Fat Pee said.

"Everything alright out there?" De'Quan asked.

"Yeah. A few trips in and out, but other than that, everything looks cool", Fat Pee reported.

"Where you at?" De'Quan asked.

"The payphone a few blocks from the spot. I'm about to bounce", Fat Pee said.

"Okay. We'll meet you at the crib", De'Quan said as the other line beeped on the phone. De'Quan clicked over and he was greeted by a pre-recorded message. "You have a call from an upstate correctional facility, caller your name...Pop. If you wish to accept these charges, please press 555".

De'Quan pressed the numbers and the line clicked over. "What's up Pop?"

"Quan, how's my b-boy doing?"

"I'm okay, just holding Mama K and them down today", De'Quan said feeling good inside to hear his father's voice.

Pop smiled, "That's good. That's good, have you been keeping your nose clean out there?"

De'Quan said, "Yeah, but I got so much going on that I don't know where to turn sometimes. They talking about sending Dre up-north too. That's going to kill me to have you and Dre in there".

Pop choose his words carefully, "Listen son, no matter what the outcome is in his situation, you have your brother and Pee at your side. I'm sure they have your back, and if Dre has to do some time, yah keep it true with him".

"Of course Pop", De'Quan said.

"Boy you still on my phone?" Mama K barked from one of her small aisles.

"Yeah Ma. I'm on the phone with your husband", De'Quan said with a chuckle.

Pop said, "Next time she comes to see me, I want you to come too. This phone thing ain't cool, and Mama K be beefing about the bill sometimes like I'm not the one who is paying for it".

They shared a laugh and De'Quan said, "Okay Pop. Hold on, let me give Ma the phone". When De'Quan put down the receiver and turned his back Meika came around the counter and picked it up.

"Hi Daddy!"

De'Quan and Dre stayed until Mama K closed the store and they made sure she and Meika were safely home. Then they went off to Dre's house to have their late night meeting.

Sitting in Dre's room De'Quan thought he should drop a bomb on Fat Pee and Dre before they get into the business at hand.

"I was talking to Ne'Sean the other night and he wants to get down with us".

Fat Pee looked over to Dre who looked shocked by this news. "I thought about it and I think we should pull him in", De'Quan said.

"Quan you sure? I mean, we talking about robbery with a mixture of other things in there. That can be some heavy shit on a nigga mind man", Fat Pee said with a lot of skepticism in his voice.

"I know, but he stepped to me and reminded me of the fact that we may be losing Dre for a minute, and it would be good to have extra hands on deck that we trust", De'Quan said as he got up and began to pace the room.

"What if Pop finds out?" Dre asked.

"How he gonna do that?" De'Quan shot back and lit up a cigarette.

Fat Pee said, "Shit man, the nigga got eyes all over the place. He might not be watching you that hard cause you the oldest, but he might be watching Sean".

De'Quan said, "He hasn't found out about us, if he did, oldest or not, he would have step to me. So adding Ne'Sean to the team shouldn't be a problem. This won't stop his basketball move and we won't let it. But the nigga is old enough to make his own decisions and we fuck around and do need him".

Dre spoke first, "Man it's on you. If you want to do it, then I guess it's cool".

They looked over to Fat Pee. He took a deep breath than shook his head, "Okay".

De'Quan put his cigarette out and said, "Fuck it, it's on then. Now what's up with this next bird?"

"Dude be in and out a lot, but what drug dealer isn't. Tasha comes and goes, and from the looks of it she has her own key now", Fat Pee said of his latest update.

Dre said, "Damn she works fast. She must have that superhead or something".

Fat Pee chuckled and said, "Word. Anyway, the family downstairs is deep and the traffic with them is all day. By about 7 or 8 o'clock that shit slows down though".

"Sounds kind of tricky", De'Quan said. "So what yah think is a good way of sliding in and out of there?"

"I think we can lay for the nigga on the stairs, and when he opens the door we'll be up close and personal with that heat in his face", Fat Pee said.

Dre smiled and said, "I like that shit. The nigga be in and out, so when he comes out we'll be waiting for his ass. And peep it, if the bitch Tasha shows up on the stairs before he opens the door, then we just put the heat to her neck and take the keys from her and walk right in".

"That will be proper", De'Quan added. "If we got the keys, he is going to think we Tasha, catching his ass off guard. You sure she's the only one with the keys Pee?"

"As far as I've seen, yeah, I mean don't get it twisted I saw dude bring other chicks there, but the only one I've seen come alone and dig for keys is Tasha", Fat Pee said.

De'Quan said, "Fuck it then, we go in tomorrow night. I'll talk to Ne'Sean and bring him with me".

Dre smiled for the first time in their meeting and said, "Good. Now let's go get some of that sticky and find some chicks".

"Word", Fat Pee said as their meeting concluded and they headed out into the dark streets.

Chapter 19

Fat Pee stole a Ford Explorer from the Corona section of Queens, and then drove to 102street and Otis Avenue to pick up De'Quan, Dre and a nervous Ne'Sean. When Fat Pee pulled up pumping Funk Master Flex on Hot 97, they came out of the shadows and piled into the jeep.

"Yo man, turn that shit off!" Dre snarled from the back seat.

"Calm down, I had to make it look good while I was stuck in traffic on 108street", Fat Pee said as he turned the radio off.

Fat Pee drove down four blocks and parked on the corner of Otis Avenue and Xenia Street. He cut the engine off and they all sat there in silence watching the late night calm of the dark street.

"Check your shit", De'Quan said, breaking the silence. Everyone in the car quickly checked their guns one last time before they slid out of the car. De'Quan and Dre headed for the house, while Ne'Sean took up his position a few houses away in the shadows. Ne'Sean was instructed to wait 20 minutes, then come in the house and wait with them on the stairs. Fat Pee remained in the car and watched the streets.

The front door of the house was unlocked giving De'Quan and Dre the easy access they needed to get in. De'Quan went into the house first, with Dre close on his heels. They crept to the staircase and were happy to hear the family on the first make enough noise to cover any creeks the staircase might have made. They made their way up to the third floor landing without incident, and were greeted by music coming from Shaborn's apartment. De'Quan shook his head thinking they could have come in there pissy drunk, knocking over everything and nobody would have heard them anyway.

Dre put his ear to the door and took a quick listen. He could hear someone talking over the steady rhythm of the music, but he only heard one voice. Dre looked at De'Quan and gave him he's on the phone signal. De'Quan nodded and they relaxed a little, staying on the ready in case the door suddenly open.

While watching the street Fat Pee saw a cab pull up to the front of the house and Tasha climbed out of the back with her hands full with shopping bags. She stood by the cab driver window and paid him. Ne'Sean stood in the shadows watching the whole transaction. His heart was racing a hundred miles a minute. He knew they were going to tie Tasha up with Shaborn if she was in the house, but they did not tell Ne'Sean what to do if Tasha showed up while he was still outside.

Tasha said good night to the cab driver and made her way to the house. Ne'Sean found himself stuck, as he watched the cab pull away from the curb and drive off. Tasha pushed open the front door and pushed it close with her foot as she turned on her heels and tugged her heavy bags up the stairs.

Ne'Sean snapped out of his trance and sprinted to the front door. He took a deep breath and turned the knob. When he stepped inside Ne'Sean could hear Tasha making her way up the stairs. With the quickness of a cheetah, he quietly began to climb the stairs after her.

Dre and De'Quan locked eyes when they heard someone coming up the stairs with shopping bags in their hands. De'Quan pointed to a corner and Dre slid into the dark space. De'Quan stepped back onto the part of the staircase that ascended to the roof of the house.

Tasha walked up the steps, digging in her Gucci bag looking for her keys when she felt someone coming up the stairs behind her. Tasha tried to turn around, but it was too late, they pounced on her before she could realize what was happening.

Ne'Sean hit her in the back of her neck with the butt of his gun causing Tasha to let out an 'Ohhh', before she semi-blacked out. As she fell forward, Dre quickly jammed his gun in her mouth with enough force to break 5 of her teeth. The music was playing so loud in Shaborn's apartment, he never Tasha cry out in pain from the two hits she took.

She tried to focus as her eyes locked eyes with Dre's. "Shhh", Dre motioned with his free hand middle finger to his lips.

De'Quan snatched her Gucci bag and fished out Tasha's baby 380. All hope Tasha had left shivered right out her body. Dre grabbed Tasha by her collar and lifted her off of the floor with the gun still in her mouth. De'Quan fished the house keys out of her bag and dropped the useless bag on the floor.

Ne'Sean climbed the rest of the stairs giving Tasha a full view of her captures. Recognition of all three of their faces made Tasha break down and she began to cry. De'Quan stepped up to her left ear and in a calm, but sinister voice he said, "Tasha, shut the fuck up with all that crying and tell me what keys open this door".

Tasha gave him a stubborn look. Dre cocked the hammer back on his 9mm to show how real they were.

"Again, what key is it?"

She pointed to two keys on the ring. Before De'Quan put the key in the door, he looked over to Ne'Sean, who gave him his nod of assurance to go ahead. Very slowly and quietly, De'Quan slid the first key into the lock and unlocked it. He put the second key in and unlocked it. He listened for any movement and didn't feel any. He readied his 9mm then pushed open the door.

De'Quan and Ne'Sean rushed into the house and found themselves in the kitchen. They ran blindly through the loud music, quickly checking any empty room then turning to a second bedroom. When they ran up in the room Shaborn was lying on his back on the bed, with his eyes closed. A big titty Spanish mommy was riding him reverse cowgirl style. She looked to be in pure ecstasy, until De'Quan punched her in her face knocking her right off of Shaborn's dick and into the corner of the room. She let out a little scream which caused De'Quan to rush her and hit her over the head with the butt of his gun.

Shaborn laid there in shock for a second, then snapped out of it when he saw De'Quan pistol whip his girl into submission. Shaborn reached for something on the side of his bed and Ne'Sean jumped right on the bed to stop him. Ne'Sean kicked Shaborn in his neck causing him to drop what he was reaching for and cry out in pain.

Ne'Sean didn't stop with his foot assault on Shaborn as he continued to kick him until he lost his footing on the bed and tumbled to the floor.

Ne'Sean quickly scrambled to his feet, as Shaborn tried to gather himself, but Shaborn was too out of it. Ne'Sean hit him over his head with his gun, than shoved it in Shaborn's mouth to stop his screaming. Once they got things under control, De'Quan silently thanked Shaborn for having the music on too loud and living on top on an empty apartment.

Dre brought Tasha into the house, locked the door and sat her on the couch. When he took the gun out of her mouth, Tasha spit blood and teeth on the floor, than she started sobbing, "Dre, what the fuck is going on? Why is yah doing this?"

"Tasha just be easy and shut up. Once we get what we came for, we outta here", he said. Dre grabbed a t-shirt from off of a chair and wiped the blood off of his gun.

De'Quan came out into the livingroom dragging the naked unconscious Spanish girl by her arms. He dragged her over to the love seat and gave up on trying to put her in it. Tasha's facial expression went from scared to angry in a New York minute, "What the fuck! What the fuck is going on here?"

Ne'Sean brought Shaborn out into the livingroom butt naked with the gun still in his mouth. When Shaborn locked eyes with Tasha, he wanted to turn back around and run back into the bedroom.

Ne'Sean pushed Shaborn onto the couch next to Tasha, who stared him down and wasted no time with the questions, "Who the fuck is this?"

Shaborn just stared at her bleeding face with a blank expression. Tasha caught the whole livingroom off guard by smacking Shaborn and screaming in his face, "Answer me dickhead!" she barked, with tears streaming down her cheeks.

De'Quan grabbed her by her arm and pulled her off of the couch, "Chill the fuck out Tasha".

He moved her to an empty chair before she really went off on Shaborn, and Dre quickly pulled out the duck tape. The first thing that had to be taped up was Tasha's mouth because she wouldn't stop crying.

As Tasha was getting taped up, De'Quan got busy with tying up the unconscious Spanish. Shaborn's mind started to click and spoke for the first time, "Wait a minute, how the fuck do you know her name?"

Dre turned from what he was doing and smacked Shaborn so hard Ne'Sean thought his hand had to be broke. "Shut the fuck up. No talking unless spoken too".

Dre finished taping Tasha up and all she did was cry and sob the whole time. He brushed it off and duck taped Shaborn's hands and feet together. When he finished Dre told Ne'Sean to watch them while he and De'Quan searched the house.

After five minutes of this, Dre got frustrated went over to Shaborn. He ripped the tape off of his mouth and said, "I'm tired of this, where's the stash at Sha?"

"I don't have a stash dawg".

That answer awarded Shaborn another hard smack to the face. Tasha gave a mumbled cheer of triumph under her taped mouth. Dre said, "You know what Sha", and put the tape back on his mouth.

Dre turned to Tasha and said, "Listen Tasha, we didn't expect for you to be in the middle of this, and I know you didn't expect to catch this lame getting his dick suck tonight either. So how about we call it even and you tell me where the shit is at, and we might even piece you off".

Tasha's eyes lit up and she nodded her head. Shaborn mumbled a strong 'bitch' from behind his taped mouth. Dre smirked at Shaborn and took the tape off of Tasha's mouth. She spit out a glob of blood in Shaborn's direction and said, "It's under refrigerator!"

"Thank You", Dre said with a smile, and then walked off toward the kitchen. He called out to De'Quan but the music was still blaring through the house.

De'Quan finally came out of the back room with a bag full of jewelry, a few guns, and a couple of gees he found in the closet.

"Yo I didn't find any work in there", De'Quan said with a frustrated look on his face.

"That's because it's under the frig", Dre said.

They went into the kitchen and De'Quan open the refrigerator door. They took everything out until De'Quan noticed something about the bottom of the refrigerator. He pulled on it until it clicked and he pulled the make shift door open. He pulled out three kilos of cocaine and a bundle of money plastic wrapped together.

"Yeah, now that's what I'm talking about", De'Quan was beaming as he looked up to his friend.

"Now let's set their asses on fire and bounce".

Dre said, "What about Tasha? I told her we would piece her off if she told me where the stash was at".

"Yeah right", De'Quan said, and then he turned to a knife set that was on the counter and snatched one out of its holder. "Piece her off with this. We can't leave that bitch alive son, you know that".

Dre scratched his head and said, "You right. She doesn't have any teeth anymore anyway. Let's stab them and set this place on fire".

"Word that sounds like a plan", De'Quan agreed and they went to work.

Dre found some oil in the cabinet and De'Quan turned on the gas burners. They went back into the livingroom and walked into Tasha giving the now woke Spanish girl an ear full.

"Bitch who the fuck is you? And why is you up in my bed sucking on my mans dick?"

The girl couldn't respond because of the tape on her mouth, but that didn't stop her from trying as she mumbled her responses. The whole scene had been making Ne'Sean nervous. He told Tasha the chill more than five times already and he didn't know what to do next. When his brother and Dre came back into the livingroom, Ne'Sean felt a sigh of relief rush over his body.

The sight of them made Tasha calm down for a minute and the only thing moving was the CD changer that had R-Kelly's 12play on heavy rotation. De'Quan stepped to Tasha and said, "Okay boys and girls, it's time to go. I heard you were promised a piece of this".

Before Tasha could answer him, De'Quan pulled the knife from behind his back and slashed her throat wide open. Ne'Sean and Shaborn watched the scene in shock as the Spanish girl started screaming under the duck tape. Dre quickly went to work on her with his knife to shut her up for good.

"Here Sean, finish dude off", De'Quan said handing his brother the knife. Ne'Sean stood there wide eyed with his nerves shaking like a pair of dice. He only wanted to take the knife because his brother was telling him to take it, but his body felt froze to the floor.

De'Quan walked closer to his brother and said, "Listen Sean, they saw our faces, and Tasha knew where we from. Now stab him and let's go".

Ne'Sean slowly took the knife out if his brother hand and stared down into Shaborn's pleading eyes. De'Quan took the gun out of Ne'Sean hand so he could focus on the task at hand.

"Yo come on Ne'Sean, do this nigga and let's go. This place is going up in flames in a minute", Dre said as he doused the couch with the kitchen oil.

Ne'Sean nervously looked from Dre back to Shaborn. Without wasting another moment on his thoughts, Ne'Sean lashed out and stabbed Shaborn in his chest. Shaborn's eyes grew wide in fright as he felt his life slowly slipping away from him. Ne'Sean left the knife in his chest as he stepped back.

"Let's go!" Dre barked as his pulled out his lighter and set the couch on fire.

Fat Pee patiently held his position on the corner of the block. He had a clear view of the house and everything looked cool to him until he saw a spark of flames in the third floor window. Fat Pee quickly started up the car and drove straight to the front of the house.

Ne'Sean was the first one to appear out the front door. He ran straight for the back door of the jeep, hoped in and slid over to give Dre the room he needed to hop in behind him and slam the door. De'Quan jumped into the front seat with their bag of goods, slammed his door and Fat Pee peeled off from the curb in a hurry. He blew the stop sign on the corner, made a quick right and headed straight for the Long Island expressway. Two blocks away Fat Pee could hear the faint sounds of sirens coming his way, but thoughts of those sirens coming for them was the furthest thing on Fat Pee's mind, as he hit the ramp at 45mph and cruised into ongoing traffic heading for the Brooklyn-Queens expressway.

Chapter 20

Fat Pee weaved the Explorer through the light late night traffic, as Ne'Sean stared out his window trying to get a grip on what he just witnessed. His brother, Dre and Fat Pee were laughing about what they just did, as De'Quan gave his version of the scene to fill Fat Pee in.

"Yo Tasha sees me dragging the bitch out of the back room and she looks at duke and says, 'who the fuck is that?' Yo Pee, you had to see the look on son face".

"Word?" Fat Pee says as they share a round of laughs from the amusing scene.

Dre caught his wind and said, "Word son! Homeboy looked like he literally shitted on himself when he saw Tasha sitting there".

"Word, and when he didn't answer her, she smacked the shit out of him!" De'Quan said as the three friends howled in pleasure.

Ne'Sean sat motionless staring out the window at the passing scenery trying to figure out what the hell was so funny. He was scared out of his mind and it could clearly be seen if someone was looking at him, but no one paid Ne'Sean any attention. Or so he thought.

"Yo Pee get off at Washington Ave", De'Quan said as he fished out a cigarette and lit it up. Getting off the highway wasn't a part of the plan knew anything about, but they stop questions De'Quan when he made sudden movements without informing the rest of them.

Fat Pee drove down the bumpy Brooklyn-Queens expressway and took his exit on their left. "Make a left at the light", De'Quan instructed as everyone sat in silence.

Fat Pee made the left, drove down two blocks then was ordered to make a right. They drove down the side of a school that was connected to a park that had some dark patches in it from bad lighting. "Pull over Pee".

When he pulled over, De'Quan hopped out of the jeep and pulled open the back passenger door, "Come on Sean".

Ne'Sean looked at Dre and Fat Pee with a hundred questions in his eyes, but he couldn't fix the words to come out. Ne'Sean just shook his head and slowly got out of the jeep.

"Wait for me on the benches", De'Quan said to Ne'Sean, who walked off without saying a word.

When his brother walked away, De'Quan stuck his head in the window and said, "Pee drop Dre off with the bag and dump this jeep. We'll meet up at Dre's house in the morning. I need to talk to Sean for a while, feel me", De'Quan said informing his partners of his change their after work plan.

"It looks like this shit is eating him up", Dre said with a worried look on his face.

"It's okay, I got this. Pee, don't forget to wipe this jeep down", De'Quan said as he gave each one a pound.

"I won't, come on Dre, get in the front. Fuck you think I am, your chauffeur or something", Fat Pee said.

When De'Quan reached his brother in the park, Ne'Sean was staring down at some ants making their way around his feet in the dark. De'Quan pulled out a Philly blunt and began to split it open.

"You can let it out anytime you ready. This blunt should be ready in a minute", De'Quan said with a taste of humor in his voice. At that moment it began to sink in how much De'Quan was beginning to grow into a young Pop.

"Quan, we didn't have to do that to Tasha".

De'Quan concentrated on putting the bag of weed on the waiting Philly in the dimly lit park. A properly rolled blunt would make his conversation with Ne'Sean go over a little smoother, than if they were sober. He could tell his little brother was caught up in his feelings at the moment and he needed to work those bad vibes out of him before they went home for the night.

"Quan seriously, what the fuck happen up there, you didn't tell me we were doing any of that", Ne'Sean said with some anger in his voice.

De'Quan lit up the blunt and sat down on the bench next to his brother. He took a strong pull off of the blunt, exhaled, and said, "Sean I told you we were into some serious things. Not any video game shit. This is what life out on the streets is about, and bottom line – Real Always Wins. Real smart, real gangster and real survival. It's hell out here some days and I don't want you riding with us if it's going to fuck you up in the end.

"We do this now to survive, but you the family's future. Just like the store is Pop's vision. Well that vision would've burned up in that fire at Grand-Ma house. I gave Mama K our stash to hold her down so she could get the store popping. That's real. We not out here doing this shit for fun. Niggas is trying to keep their heads above water, before these projects or streets drown us".

De'Quan passed his brother the blunt, than stood up and started pacing. Ne'Sean took his pulls of the blunt and tried to see the game through his brother eyes.

De'Quan continued, "Tasha knew who we were, and where we lived. Either that nigga she was fucking would have grew some balls or made her talk or she would have told the police about us. She was a good bitch, but a bitch with too much power over us and our situation. We can't risk letting people know who we are and what we do. That puts us in danger and Mama K and Meika, you feel me".

Ne'Sean felt his brother passion as he looked up from the ground and into his eyes. "Quan I love you and I will do anything to help us survive out here while Pop is away. I'm not going to lie, that thing had me messed up, but like you said 'it was either them or us".

"That's what I'm talking about Sean. People out here ain't trying to give us or Mama K shit, but they claim to have love for Pop. Those motherfuckers don't give a fuck if we starve to death in that house. That's real".

De'Quan's words and the blunt began to take its effects on Ne'Sean as he said, "You right. I just didn't know killing someone was a part of it".

De'Quan sat back down next to his brother and said, "Sean I will do anything out here to make sure yah safe, even if that means killing the only witness to our crime".

"I guess you right. You know I will always have your back out here. I know things have been hard on Mama K since Pop been gone. So any help she can get from us is good, right", Ne'Sean said.

De'Quan smiled and said, "Right. So you with me".

Ne'Sean sucked his teeth and said, "Yeah man".

"Good, now let's walk. We have to find a cab on the boulevard or something", De'Quan said, leading the way out of the park.

"Quan, how long niggas plan on doing this for?" Ne'Sean asked.

"Shit, after tonight's hit we might be good until you get that first NBA check, you know what I'm saying", De'Quan said giving his brother a pound. He got a new rush of energy just thinking about counting the money they took.

$$\ast\ast\ast\ast\ast$$

It was dark in his room as Ne'Sean stared up at the ceiling with images of the scene in Queens riding his thoughts. He tried to block it out and think about the future. This thing with De'Quan wasn't forever. Once he got his basketball scholarship, he will go to college and hopefully the pros. Those are the thought's he wanted to close his eyes with, not Tasha and Shaborn's face. Faces he knew he would never forget.

Chapter 21

The line in front of Brooklyn criminal court was extremely long and not moving fast enough. Dre found himself ready to walk off the line and say 'catch me when you can' on his way back to Marcy. He knew he would have to come up with a good story to tell his mother and Mama K when they question about what happen at court today, and he didn't have one. Without a good creditable story, he stuck on the slow moving line with De'Quan and Rahkem feeling as nervous as he was.

The three friends made it through the metal detector without incident and checked the docket list to find the courtroom. When they reached the courtroom, Dre spotted his lawyer talking to another white man in a suit.

"There he go right there", Dre said and they made their in his direction.

When Mr. Massinger saw Dre and his small entourage coming his way he cut his conversation short and guided the group over to the side. Dre picked up Mr. Massinger after firing Mr. Gordon for trying to get him to take 1-3years upstate.

"Mr. Jones how are you today?" The lawyer asked as he shook Dre's hand.

"Listen Mr. Massinger, what's the judge going to say today?" Dre said skipping the formalities.

Mr. Massinger thought to himself 'okay', and got right to it. "Well the district attorney is being generous today, so I got him down to six months with five years probation when you get out. I think it's a good deal, being that you were arrested red handed with the gun, and you have no pyres".

Rahkem jumped in and said, "Then why can't he get a straight five years probation without the six months, since he ain't never been arrested".

Mr. Massinger looked over to Rahkem and thought he should choose his words wisely. "Because the D.A.'s office wants him to do some type of jail time. I was just talking to Mr. Crossmen and he won't go down any further, and since trial is out of the question, I say take the deal and run".

De'Quan said, "Can we get a minute here", and pulled Dre over to the side with Rahkem on their heels.

"So what you want to do bro?" De'Quan asked Dre.

Dre mind was spinning, as he looked around at all the confusion going on in the courthouse hallway. People were barking orders at their lawyers or on the pay phones, court officer's dragging handcuffed people in and out of courtrooms, and someone's baby would not stop crying.

He sucked his teeth and said, "I can do six months, as long as I know yah going to hold me down".

"Of course we got you", De'Quan said. Rahkem nodded in agreement.

Dre thought for a moment then said, "Fuck it. As long as I don't have to go in today, and we should try to get that probation off too".

Rahkem said, "Shit, that cracker can get you at least 30 days out on the streets for some party and bullshit. If not we wildin on him in this hallway".

Rahkem was big for 17, standing at 6'3 and weighing 210 pounds. He would use his size when he needed too, especially on white people. However, to get him to run up in a spot to do a robbery was a whole another thing. Rahkem was too soft for a real drama scene.

They walked back over to Mr. Massinger with Rahkem stepping a little closer to the lawyer than he was before. Dre said, "I'll take some time, but I don't want any probation, and I'm not going in today".

Mr. Massinger looked at all three faces and quickly realized Dre wasn't asking him to make it happen. He was telling him to make it happen. "Oh okay, I'm going to see about getting you the straight jail time. The judge won't sentence you today anyway, that won't happen until probably next month. I'll go inside and talk to Mr. Crossmen and I should have this straighten out in ten minutes so you won't have to wait around all day", the lawyer said then ran off.

Dre left the court house feeling relived the judge gave him some more time to smell the fresh city air before they took him in for his bid. They hailed a cab and piled into the back.

"Dre, you think your moms will let us throw a party?' Rahkem asked as the cab weaved through traffic.

"Yeah that sounds like a good idea", De'Quan added.

"I don't know, but I'll talk to my sister. She'll take care of my moms'".

"Yeah, so it's on, I'm going to get my cousin Dog Time from Queens to DJ for us", Rahkem said excited.

"Your cousin who? Never heard of him", De'Quan said and Dre started laughing in Rahkem's face.

Rahkem smiled and said, "Okay, laugh now, but I'm telling you my cousin is going to be big time. You watch".

Chapter 22

"A Tammy, wait up a minute".

Tammy stopped to see who was trying to hold up her progress and was surprised when she saw it was Dre.

Tammy's insides lit up, but she tried to keep a straight face when she said, "Oh hi Dre, I have to go to the store for my mom, so she'll get off of my back".

Dre smiled and said, "Can I walk with you then?"

"If you want", Tammy said nonchalantly.

They headed up to Marcy Avenue with Dre watching Tammy out the corner of his eye. He found himself trying to put together a set of words that wouldn't make him look uncool. Dre never had any problems bagging a female. It was Tammy.

Tammy Brown was labeled in the hood as hard2get. Her chocolate complexion, chinky eyes, and long Indian hair made her a prize to bag on the streets, but whenever someone tried to rap to Tammy, she always claimed to have no time to stop. Dre figured walking with her would give him some time to get in her ear.

"You know, you shouldn't be walking around here by yourself anyway. Where's your man at?" Dre asked. It was too much talk on the streets; he needed to get his info straight from the source.

Tammy snickered and rolled her eyes, "what man?"

Dre felt his stock rise as he said, "the one I thought I peeped lurking around your building. I guess I was hallucinating".

Tammy smiled, but remained silent. Tammy thought she was the only one watching him. To hear Dre say he be watching her made Tammy feel good inside. Watching Dre from the corner of her eyes Tammy could feel the butterflies in her stomach working over time. She tried to relax so she wouldn't look to anxious as they walked up the long block.

"So, what you been up too Tammy, I haven't seen you in a while", Dre said after their awkward silence.

"I be in the house a lot. When I'm not here, I'm at my cousin house in Williamsburg. Ain't much in Marcy for me", she dryly stated.

"How do you know if you don't stick around to see?" Dre asked.

Tammy cracked a smile and said, "you might be right about that. What about you, where you be at?"

"Trying to lay low, shit is getting a little crazy out here. So I've been just trying to stay busy in my own little world", Dre said with a smile.

When they reached the store on Marcy Avenue, a small dice game was in full swing out front of the store. "What you got to get?" Dre asked her.

"Some milk and female things", Tammy said.

"Female things? I'll wait for you out here than", Dre said giving Tammy her privacy.

"Dre what's happening?" A light skin brother said he was watching the dice game from the background.

Dre stepped over and gave him a pound, "What up Tone, why you not playing?" Tone was a notorious dice player in the hood.

"Shiittt, not today. I got to finish this pack and head uptown, you feel me. Yo what's up with you and Tammy?" Tone asked as his eyes scanned the traffic rolling down Marcy Avenue.

"Yeah! 4, 5, 6 pay up motherfucker's!"

Dre thought about his answer and figured it would be good to put it out there for the wolves to back off. "Yeah that's about to be me", Dre said confidently. "So yah niggas back up off of that". Dre and Tone shared a laugh and gave each other a pound.

"It's all good homie. She's definitely a banger", as soon as Tone finished his sentence a crack head walked up on them.

"Tone I need four".

Tone did a quick look around and said, "Good, go around the corner".

"Tone I'll get wit you later", Dre said.

Tone wasn't listening his mind was on his business as he trailed the crack head around the corner.

"Okay bitches, make daddy proud", someone barked from the dice game as he shook the dice and rolled them out of his hand in a smooth motion.

Dre snapped out of watching the game when Tammy came out of the store stuffing her change in her purse. Dre took her bag from her to carry the load back to the building. On the walk back Dre told himself it was now or never and said, "Tammy can I take you out tonight, to eat or something. I'm type hungry and that will give us some sit down time, if you don't mind that of course".

Tammy was a little taken aback by this. She thought he would just ask her for her number and run off. "Well I... When I drop this stuff to my mom I'll see".

"We can go to Junior's, so tell your moms I'll pick her up a cheesecake. How about that?" Dre said with a smile. Nobody's mother is going to turn down free cheesecake from Junior's.

She smiled and said, "That might do it. Moms loves her some cheesecake".

They chuckled and Dre said, "While you up there call a cab, so she won't think I'm trying to kidnap her daughter".

She laughed and said, "Kidnap huh, I'm not worried about you. I can handle myself".

Dre had to laugh at her toughness. "Okay gangstress. I don't want any problems. I just want to eat and get to know who the real Tammy is".

She stayed quiet as his words rolled around in her head. She took the bag from him and said, "I'll be right back".

Dre sat on the back upright of the bench in front of Tammy's building and began to think about how he was going to incorporate Tammy into his near future plans. Dre knew he couldn't do a bid with the average bird from the projects holding him down. The thought has been on his mind ever since he agreed to take the short bid, to find a girl that would hold him down.

Dre had his eye on Tammy for some time, but he could never catch her at a good time. A shot rang out in the early night sky, invading Dre's thoughts of Tammy. From the sound of the shot, it came from the direction of the dice game. Dre shook his head and checked his hip to reassure himself of having his own peacemaker, then turned his thoughts back to the chocolate beauty he was going to make his official wifey.

When Tammy finally came out the front door of the building, she was wearing a blue Nike jacket to go with the blue Nike track suit she was rocking. Dre liked what he was seeing.

"My mom said, make sure that cheesecake got a lot of cherries on it", Tammy said, smiling as they hopped into the cab.

"Yes ma'am", Dre said with a chuckle.

On the way there, they talked about music and the latest videos out. When the cab pulled up to Junior's it was a regular car show outside. Three different sound systems were banging three different songs at the same damn time. Rims were gleaming and the chicks were out in full force trying to bag them a balla for the night.

Dre and Tammy sat in a corner booth and scanned their menus. "What you want to eat?"

Tammy looked up from her menu and said, "I'm not really hungry. I just want a cheeseburger and fries".

The waitress popped up and Dre gave her Tammy's order, with a soda, and he ordered a chicken cutlet parmesan, and fruit juice. "Oh and let me get a cheesecake with lots of cherries to go please", Dre said with a wide grin.

"Thank you", Tammy said soft enough for only Dre to hear her.

While they waited for their food to come Dre asked, "What you going to do after high school, this your last year right?"

"Yeah, I was thinking about going to an all black college down south. But I be worrying about leaving my mom in Marcy by herself".

"You don't have any brothers or sisters in another Boro or something?" Dre asked.

Tammy chuckled, "What you mean like the Ricki Lake show?"

They shared a laugh and she said, "Nah it's just me and my mom. I got cousins I hang out with, but I guess that's not the same. What about you, what you going to do?"

Dre said, "I'm done with school. I copped my G.E.D. so that's the end of that. I don't know what I'm going to do though. I'll have some time to think about it".

She skipped pass his last statement and said, "Sooo, what's up with you and Kimmie?"

The question caught Dre off guard for a second. He didn't let it show as he kept a straight face and said, "Me and Kimmie been old news. How do you say – we had a conflict of interest".

Tammy already knew all of this; she just wanted to hear it from him. Tammy had been keeping light tabs on Dre, so she knew more about him than he thought.

Dre stared across the table and told himself to put all his cards on the table and see how it goes. "Tammy, I know we only know each other from passing in the projects, but I'm feeling

123

your vibe, and I would like to get to know you better than the average everyday p.j. life".

She smiled and said, "You mean we be exclusive".

Dre said, "No pressure. But I am feeling you like that".

Tammy blushed hard, but kept her eyes focused on her soda as she rubbed her finger over the top of the glass. She could feel his eyes burning a hole in her forehead.

"I'm feeling you too Dre, but I don't want to be apart no sideline drama. If it's going to be me and you, than we can swing that and see how it goes. But please Dre", she paused and looked up into his eyes. "Don't play me like I'm one of these lames out here with no future plans or anything like that".

Dre felt her sincerity and knew his gut feeling was right about her. "Come on Tammy, if you got my back, than I got your front".

She giggled, "Got my front huh. What's that some new slang or something".

"I can show you better than I can tell you".

Their food came and Dre sat back to see how Tammy would eat in front of him. If she picked at her food like a bird, then she was fronting. Dre wasn't surprised to see Tammy throw ketchup on her burger and fries, and dig right into it like he wasn't there.

By the end of their meal, both of them were feeling good about each other. They talked about everything except the fact that Dre only had 25days left out on the streets, and what he and his friends did for money. By the time they got out of the cab in front of Tammy's building the vibe between them was strong. Dre choose to ride with her up on the elevator. That's where he made his move and kissed Tammy until they missed her floor twice.

"Call me around 2 when I get home from school", Tammy said as she stepped off of the elevator.

"A'ight", Dre said as he kissed her one last time. His mind was already made up; he would go up to her school and pick her up instead of calling. Now that's official.

Chapter 23

With his head spinning out of control with crazy thought's, Dre found himself waking up every day and staring at the calendar on the wall. Ten more days before his final court date and it felt like those last hours were closing in fast on Dre. Some days he woke up and felt like running from New York City and its twisted system, but then the realization of not having anywhere to go would seep in.

Dre got up and went down the hallway to the bathroom. He cut the shower on and heard the phone in his room ringing.

"Hello".

"Hey you. I just wanted to see if you was up yet", Tammy said beaming through the phone.

"I'm getting in the shower now. I'll be over there when I'm done", Dre said.

"Oh so you're in your birthday suit and wet right now", Tammy said with a snicker in her voice.

Dre laughed, "Yes sexy. Now make sure you ready when I get there please".

"Okay...okay. I'll be ready".

They hung up and Dre jumped into the shower. Thoughts of Tammy seemed to be the only Dre could think about lately. All of the bad questions would flood his mind and he would have to shake it off. Will she do the bid with me? Of course, she will, she's feeling me like that. Will Tammy mess around on me with another guy? Naw, I'll just have my boys keep an eye on her. Dre smiled to himself in the shower; yeah Tammy is going to hold me down while I'm gone.

He finished in the bathroom, went into his room and lit up a half of blunt while he threw on something to wear. Dark green Polo jeans, Nike shirt, some dark green Nike A.C.G.'s and a Nike hat to match rounded out his Saturday outfit. Dre grabbed $2,300.00 and his 9mm out of the stash spot, and he was gone.

When Tammy open the door, Dre found himself breathing again. It seem like all of the drama he went through in his house and in the streets just disappeared. Tammy was the type of girl who could make a Gap suit look like a Parda suit.

Tammy loved looking her best everyday she spent with Dre and this day wasn't any different. She put on a big smile then step to the side so Dre could come in. She made a motion and said, "You like it?"

"You looking tasty in that skirt", Dre said.

"Oh ok, I thought I was going to have to put on something else", Tammy said.

Dre chuckled as he plop down on the couch, "Oh no you not. You look good Tam. Seriously baby".

Tammy looked in the mirror and said, "I guess. So I saw the shoes I want to get today in a store on Fulton".

"It don't look like you need any more shoes to me", Dre said as Tammy open the hallway closet revealing a stack of shoe boxes and coats.

Tammy fumbled in the closet for a moment than said, "Shut up silly. I need a pair of shoe to go with the outfit I'm wearing to your party. And for your information I got money to buy my shoes".

"If you got money, then can I get a pair of shoes too?" Dre said with a big smile on his face.

Tammy grabbed her purse and said, "Do unto others, what you want done for you. Let's go".

126

They walked up and down Fulton Street all day buying more stuff than they expected to get. Dre made Tammy hold onto her money and he paid for everything they picked out for the day. Tammy nothing about how or where Dre got his money, and she never asked. As long as Dre kept his focus on her and he was safe in the streets, Tammy didn't worry about anything else. She promised Dre she would come to see him when turned himself in to do his bid and the way Dre made her feel, Tammy had no thoughts of checking for another man while he was away.

The sky began to darken, so Dre took that as a sign to call it a day, grab some food and head back to Marcy. They grabbed some Chinese food and Dre stepped out onto the street to hail a cab. A brown Lincoln town car pulled over.

"Come on Tammy".

Dre open the door and the sound of someone winning some tickets on the radio flouted out of the car. Tammy jumped in and slide over in the backseat. Dre was putting the bags on the floor in the middle of the backseat when he thought he saw a glimpse of something out the corner of his eye. As Dre turned to get into the cab, he saw two guys coming at him fast. One had a big Rambo knife in his hand.

"Oh Shit!" Dre lost his balance as he tried to grab the gun off of his waist and jump into the cab at the same time.

"Yo Drive...Drive!"

The knife welding man tried to stab Dre but missed and stabbed the door panel as his partner quickly ran around to the outside and snatched open the door. "Give me the money bitch!" he barked as he grabbed Tammy's purse.

"Hey...hey!" The cab driver nervously yelled from the front seat.

Blam!

The sound was deafening in the body of the cab as the passenger side window blew out. "Oh shit, he got a gun".

"Get off of me!" Tammy cried out as she struggle with the robber for her purse.

127

The cab driver slammed down on the gas pedal, and Tammy's purse ripped right from her grip as the thirsty purse snatcher tumbled to the ground. Dre looked out the back window as the cab driver swerved through the narrow block with a purpose. The two robbers scrambled and dipped off into an alley way.

"Damn it! He got my bag Dre!"

"Damn!" Dre banged the butt of his gun on the car door as he watched the cab driver run a red light.

"Yo my man take us to 506 Park Street". Dre said through the open partition.

"Hell no. Yah are getting out of my car at the next light. I can't deal with all this shooting and shit. Look at my got damn window", the cab driver angrily barked over his shoulder as he tried to keep his eyes on the road.

"Look motherfucker, take us to Park Street. Fuck you mean you throwing us out. We got money", Dre snapped as he threw a twenty dollar bill through the partition. "Here man, keep the change. Just take us to Park man".

The cab driver pulled over at the next curb and turned to face his two passengers. "Please mister, don't leave us out here like this", Tammy pleaded.

"Who's going to pay for my damn window?"

"Man my girl just lost her bag because you was bullshitting when I told you to pull off. So who you think is going to take the biggest lost today?" Dre said.

The cab driver looked over to Tammy who had tears streaming down the side of her brown cheeks. "Okay...but yah got to get out at Park". The car skidded from the curb without the driver saying another word.

Dre turned to Tammy and hugged her, "You alright baby".

"Them niggas got my bag Dre".

"I know this shit is fucked up. I should have been more on point", Dre said feeling his anger boil in the inside.

"My keys and everything was in there. We have to tell the police", Tammy said looking up at Dre.

"We can't do that Tammy", Dre said.

"Why not Dre. They robbed us!" Tammy barked. Dre never saw Tammy this angry before and he felt lost on how to calm her down in a short period time before the cab driver officially throw's them out.

"Tammy think for a second. I just let off a shot in the back of this cab, and I'm already going to jail in a few days for another gun charge. They going to pay more attention to me, than them two crack heads that snatched your bag". Dre said in a stern but calming voice.

"I'm sorry baby, but we just going to have to take this lost", Dre said gently taking her hand into his. With his free hand, Dre whipped the tears from her cheek.

The cab driver quickly broke up their hallmark moment by abruptly pulling the cab over and saying, "Hey, this is as far as I go with you two".

Dre quickly looked out the window to see where they were, "Come on Tammy".

Dre took Tammy home and after they went through the motions with Tammy's mother about how she lost her keys, Dre said his good bye's and headed home knowing one day he will see them two crack heads again. Brooklyn was big, but not that big.

Chapter 24

"Bucktown!"

"Home of the original gun clappers!"

"Bucktown!"

"Home of the original gun clappers!"

The party goers chanted in unison with Smith & Wesson over the body popping beat. The apartment was packed and Dre party was in full swing by the 11:00p.m. hour with hustlers, back-packers, fly girl's, hot chicks from outside the project's, and the gangsters all in attendance to pay homage to a person only a quarter of the apartment knew by face.

Dre's sister Shakia put the party together and no one argued with her on how she wanted to do it big for her brother. Dre's mothers moved to and from her bedroom to the kitchen to refill her glass every once in awhile, until the liquor put her to sleep.

The only piece of furniture they left in the livingroom was the couch and the loveseat. All the rest of the furniture was divided between Dre and Shakia bedrooms. Giving the livingroom all the space it needed to house the party goers. Rahkem's cousin Dog-Time came through for the small fee of $500.00, and from the way he had the place rocking he was worth every penny.

Dre sat back on the couch with Tammy up under his arm staring out at the people partying in his name and he couldn't believe the atmosphere. "If this is how they partying when I'm going in, imaging when I come out", Dre said to Tammy.

Tammy kissed him and whispered in his ear, "Dre I want you".

Dre pulled her closer to him and kissed her hard. Tammy's temperature had been rising all day, but they never had a moment to themselves. Tammy pulled back and stood up.

Taking Dre's hand she maneuvered through the crowd and headed straight to Dre bedroom.

Dre bedroom was packed with stuff Shakia did not want broken and his bed looked like the coat rack with over twenty coats spread out across it. The only light in the room came from a lamp on an end table next to his buried bed.

Dre locked the door and put his back to it as pure lust took over them. They kissed with passion and fondled each other aimlessly until Dre stopped. Tammy thought something was wrong until he stepped over to the bed and with one sweeping motion; Dre knocked all the coats off of his bed. Dre turned to Tammy and took off his shirt. He removed her shirt and brassiere and began to suck on her awaiting nipples. Tammy laid back on the bed and let his put his tongue to work as Dre sucked on her nipples, then eased his tongue down to her panty line. He smoothly pulled down her skirt and panties at the same time then open up her legs. Tammy's pussy was throbbing before he could even breathe on it. Dre smiled to himself then dived in.

"Ooooh Dre!"

Dre went to work until he felt her legs shaking and Tammy starting calling out his name like she was in a trance. Dre quickly hopped out of his pants and boxers then entered her, as Tammy let out a soft moan. They rocked back and forth to the rhythm of the beat that was seeping through the walls, causing Tammy to get wetter and wetter with each stroke.

When Dre felt it coming, it felt too good to pull out this time. Dre climaxed and Tammy welcomed it by grabbing him by his waist and pulling him tighter. For the first time in their lives, they were one.

They laid in each other arms panting and planting soft wet kisses on each other face until Dre pulled back to look into her eyes. A tear slid out the corner of Tammy's eye and Dre caught it with a kiss, "You know I love you right".

"I love you too", she said hugging him extra tight. "I wish you didn't have to go".

Dre smiled and said, "Me too".

The shared a laugh and Dre said, "Come on, we have to get back to the party before people start asking for us".

"I know right. You wanting to be all bad and stuff".

Dre busted out laughing, "Okay I'll take the heat for it, even though I remember the story was a little bit different from that".

"Whatever".

*****
___

De'Quan figured Shakia had to be five years older than him, and that might be the reason he never paid her any attention before. Older women never appealed to him that much like a woman his own age range. So why had he been watching Shakia all night then?

Shakia was a shade lighter than Dre and that was the closest the comparison came between the brother and sister pair. She had an ass and hips that made her co-worker droll at her all day, and a set of 36c cups that men stared at while they talked her. This always pissed Shakia off. She kept her weave intact and her nails stayed done. All of this made De'Quan question himself again – Why I didn't notice her before?

De'Quan played the corners as he watched Shakia move around the apartment. Getting her groove on out on the dance floor, mingling with the people that came in and out the door, and she kept the kitchen in order with every drunk and high person in the place asking her for something to eat every five minutes. Her people skills were surprising to De'Quan who never said more than hi and bye to Shakia in all the time he and Dre had been friends.

Having eye opening thoughts about his best friend sister was beginning to freak him out. De'Quan knew he needed to talk to somebody. He made his move through the party searching for somebody he could talk too in confidence about this.

De'Quan spotted Fat Pee and Ron Ron over by the d.j. table talking to two brown sugar females and stepped over to them. Not wanting to bust their groove De'Quan stepped in and said, Hey, excuse me ladies for a second. I need to borrow Pee here for a moment and I'll send him right back".

The girl's just gave De'Quan a whatever look as he put his arm around fat Pee's neck and guided him over to the side out of ear shot.

"Yo if you wit it we can get rid of that nigga Ron Ron and take turns on them chicks", Fat Pee said as he took a sip from his drink.

"Naw man, I got a problem".

Fat Pee thought it was beef and tried to quickly sober up, "Word, where they at. We can hit them".

De'Quan cut him off, "Naw man. It ain't that".

Fat Pee began to get restless, "Well spit it out nigga. This ain't no guessing game, what's happening".

De'Quan took one last look over his shoulder before he said, "Its Shakia man. I'm thinking about pressing her tonight".

"Fuck you mean press her?" Fat Pee asked with a confused look on his face.

"Look, I know that's Dre sister. That's why I had to talk to you about it. I've been eyeing her all night. I don't know if it's the fucking liquor, or that got damn perfume she's wearing, but every time she passes me shit feels crazy man".

To Fat Pee pussy was pussy, as long as it was above age, but this was close to home looking at each other sister. "Man just ask her to dance. Can't much go down cause she sees us as broke hoodlums who don't have a dime to our names. What's the worst that can happen from a dance to get her off your mind"?

*****

Two hours later the party was at its 2:45a.m. hour and De'Quan found himself in the bathroom doing the unthinkable.

"Oh shit! Oh shit!"

"Oh Quan fuck me. Fuck me!"

'Oh Shiittt!"

The world shook as they climaxed in harmony hard enough to almost break the sink off of the wall. The air stood still for what seemed like an eternity, until De'Quan's penis got soft and it slid out of Shakia. He stepped back and she slowly hopped off of the sink. They stood there for a moment just staring at each other until she broke the silence, "We can't let Dre know this happen".

"Aww, yeah...You're right", De'Quan said as he began to pull up his pants feeling embarrassed. She was his best friend sister and here she was making him promise to keep something from him.

"I have to use the bathroom", Shakia said.

"Oh yeah. Sure. I'm sorry, female thang right. I'll go", De'Quan fumbled with his words, then quickly got scarce.

Chapter 25

Since Dre had to turn himself in De'Quan tried to keep a low profile in the projects. He didn't want anyone getting any ideas because his partner in crime was on ice for a few months. Fat Pee always did his own thing outside of him hanging out with De'Quan and Dre, so it would not surprise De'Quan when he wouldn't hear from Fat Pee for a few days that usually meant some chick had his ear and they were laying up somewhere, but the thing that was troubling De'Quan was how Ne'Sean had been acting.

Since the robbery at Shaborn's house, Ne'Sean had seemed to be more closed in. Most days he would leave before De'Quan woke up, and afterschool Ne'Sean would become MIA for hours before finally showing up at the house and going straight to bed. Mama K was to focus on getting the store off the ground and making sure Meika stayed in eye sight to pay a lot attention to Ne'Sean and his constant mood swings, but not De'Quan. He had been watching his brother and he just wasn't himself anymore.

De'Quan needed to talk to Rahkem so he told him to meet him in the park. They sat on the bench and watched Ne'Sean and Jamel play a two on two game against duo who looked like they weren't any match for the much younger teammates.

"What the fuck you mean you had to spend a thousand dollars the other day Rah?' De'Quan asked heated. "You say the shit like it's okay to spend my dough on your escapades".

Rahkem was shaken by De'Quan's outburst. He figured he could take the money out like he did before and De'Quan wouldn't think nothing of it. Ever since Dre went to jail, De'Quan had been acting real up tight.

"Quan I told you my brother was in a little trouble. You know he got a mad gambling problem, and them niggas was talking about killing him this time. That shit would break my mom's heart man if she found out I had a chance to save him and I didn't".

De'Quan lit up a cigarette and thought about what Rahkem was telling him as he kept his eyes on the basketball game.

"Rah you my man and all that, but don't try to play me son. We trusted you to hold that dough for us, and every time I turn around you got another situation going on in your crib that's costing us bread", De'Quan said clearly upset.

Sweat slid down the side of his face as he continued to explain himself, "Quan you know how my brother do. One week he's up and the next week he's fucked up. When he goes up next time, I'll make sure he puts the gee back".

De'Quan blew smoke in his face and said, "Yeah, you do that, and tell that nigga to go to AA or gamblers anonymous".

De'Quan looked back to the game just in time to see his brother score on a layup, "Yeah that's what I'm talking about".

Rahkem saw this as an opportunity to change the subject, "Yo Ne'Sean looks like he's getting better since last season".

De'Quan half listen to him, but still answered him, "Yeah, my bro is going to the pros one day".

"What's our count now Rah", De'Quan asked after a light silence.

"Like 27gees".

"You see Rah; this is where you be fucking up at. What the fuck you mean 'like'", De'Quan snapped.

"Come on Quan, it's just a roundabout number. The count is $27,670.00. Damn son, you need a blunt or something. You so uptight man".

De'Quan laughed to himself and said, "Yeah, I hear you. You better not be fucking with me Rah", and with that De'Quan hopped up off of the bench and walked across the park to the court.

"Yo time out for a second. Sean I'm about to slide for a little while".

Ne'Sean passed the ball to Jamel and said, "Time out", and walked over to brother.

"I'm going to lay up somewhere for a little while. What's up you good, you need anything".

"Naw I'm good. I'm going to play for a little while then I'm going to take a shower".

"Alight. You know if you need to talk to me I'm here for you", De'Quan said wanting to break the mood, his brother has been carrying with himself for a few months now.

"Yeah I know bro".

"Yo I need you to find out what's good with Rahkem and his brother. And see if he been spending money on any of these chicks", De'Quan. Ne'Sean was always good info on people and not being on front street while he did it.

"Okay, I got you bro", Ne'Sean said and gave him a pound. Before he ran back over to the game he said, "Oh and tell Shakia I said hi".

"How the hell you know that's where I'm going?" De'Quan asked surprise his brother knew about his secret meetings with Shakia.

"Later Bro", Ne'Sean said with a chuckle and ran back to join his game.

$$*****$$

De'Quan woke up one Sunday feeling like he needed to do something different. They had been getting away with the way they got big money in a short period of time without drawing any attention to themselves, but in order for them to really move around, they needed a vehicle to do that. If De'Quan started moving around now, by the time Dre came home, he can have something set up already.

After thinking about what he wanted to do for the day, De'Quan went into the kitchen and snuck up behind his mother.

"Muah", De'Quan planted a kiss on the side of his mother neck.

"Good morning baby".

"Ma can I borrow your car today?" De'Quan asked as he poured himself a cup of juice.

"To do what", She asked over her shoulder as she kept her eyes on the eggs she was frying.

"I want to go check something out at this store in Queens", De'Quan said as he sat down at the table.

"Check something out huh. Your check something's out be taking all night, and I want to close up the store at 8 tonight", Mama K said moving from the stove over to the counter to make their plates.

"Mama K I'll be back way before that".

"Ok, go wake your brother up", She said just as Meika shuffled into the kitchen rubbing her eyes. "Morning baby".

"Morning Mama", Meika said giving her a kiss and shuffling over to the table.

"He's not here".

"That boy left already on a Sunday", Mama K said giving them their plates.

"Nobody is in the park this early. He's probably down there shooting around", De'Quan said.

"Mama K I need some money", Meika said.

"Oh so now I'm the ATM today", Mama K said as she poured Meika a cup of juice.

"No, but it's this shirt I want to buy for school. Ma, it's only 35 dollars ", Meika said ignoring her food.

"Oh yeah Erica Cane, if it's only 35 dollars, then why don't your rich self have the money", Mama K Joked as she sat down at the table.

Meika could not start eating until she had conformation on the shirt. "Oh come on Ma, the shirt will go perfect with my D.K.N.Y. suit I want to wear. You know how it is Ma not to be matching and everybody is talking about you".

Mama K laughed and said, "So now I don't be matching and everybody be talking about me huh".

"No not you Mama. You know you the flyest mom in Brooklyn. I'm just saying, you know what I'm going through right now", Meika said.

Mama K thought for a moment then said, "Okay, I'll give you the money. But you have to go with your brother".

"What brother?" De'Quan asked with his mouth full of food.

"You...You said you're going shopping, or I should say checking things out at the store, so you can take your sister and she can grab her shirt. Everybody happy. Now Meika eat your food".

"Ma you can't be serious. Meika is going to cramp my style today", De'Quan said with a frown on his face".

"Boy you driving your Mama's car, you ain't got no style".

$$*****$$

"Where are we going Quan? I thought Mama K told you I had to buy a shirt off of Fulton", Meika said from the backseat of the car. She was steaming and wasn't afraid to let it be known.

To put Meika in the backseat, De'Quan picked up Q to take the ride with them to Queens. De'Quan figured he could put Meika in the back, turn up the music and tune her out. Today Meika wasn't having it so he had to set her straight before she really starting acting crazy.

"Look Mama K didn't say anything to me about Fulton, cause she knew I was going to Queens today. Jamaica ave got all the same stuff as Fulton street anyway, so be easy", De'Quan said as he weaved Mama K's Honda through the light Interboro traffic.

Meika huffed and puffed but kept quiet. She knew when to push her brothers buttons and when to leave him alone. De'Quan turned the music back up and they cruised to Queens.

They walked for an hour through the Coliseum and a couple of stores on 174 street until Meika found the perfect shirt.

Once he made sure his sister was straight, they got back into the car and drove down to 187 street and Jamaica avenue to 'Select your Car' dealership. When they pulled into the parking lot Meika went back into her investigative roll again.

"Why are we here? You going to buy a car?"

De'Quan laughed, "Damn little K, can I answer one question at a time".

"You are right. That's why we here, right", Meika eagerly pressed.

"Maybe, now you can stay in the car if you want, while I look around", De'Quan said as he open his door to get out the car.

"No way Jose, I'm not staying in this car if you getting one of these", Meika said hopping out of the backseat.

De'Quan heard about 'Select your Car' dealership in the hood for having a nice selection of foreign cars at low prices if you had the cash on hand. Your paperwork would be fixed and you will drive away without any problems. He wasn't too sure he would buy a car today, but just in case something caught his eye, De'Quan had $11,000 cash on him and Q who could drive his mother car back to Brooklyn.

They browsed through the car lot getting caught up in smell of every drug dealer dream sitting on chrome. B.M.W.'s, Benz's, Acura Legend's, Land Cruisers, and a few Jeep Cherokee's were just a few things they had shining on the lot.

"What type of joint you looking for?" Q asked.

"I don't know yet son, but when I see it, it'll hit me", De'Quan said as they kept walking through the aisle.

"Yeah I feel that, what about that three and a quarter over there?" Q asked.

"Yeah Quan, get a B.M.W.", Meika beamed as she stayed hot on his heels.

"Just because you want me to get one, don't mean I'm going to look good in it", De'Quan joked.

"Shit, ugly Sherry would look good in that three and a quarter", Q said.

"So what kind of car do you want?" Meika asked, and then said, "What about that red one over there?"

They walked over to the car and De'Quan felt it.

"Damn son, that shit is fly", Q said sizing the car up.

"Lexus GS300", De'Quan said as he stared at the front grill. Red with light tints on it and shiny factory rims on it. He walked over to the driver's side and scanned the price and mileage on the window.

Ron sipped on his cup of coffee and watched the lot from the confines of his office. From his window he can watch the reactions of people from afar, whether they showed interest in a particular car, or they are just browsing.

Ron watched two guys and a young girl hover around the Lexus, and thought it was time he made his move to see if their serious about it. He put down his cup, grabbed the master keys and stepped out into the lot expecting nothing, but always hoping for a sale.

"Good afternoon, my name is Ron. Can I help you?"

"My brother like this car", Meika said speaking for the small entourage.

Ron put on his winning smile and said, "Oh really".

"Yeah, looks real nice. How much are yah looking for?" De'Quan asked.

"Well this Lexus is in good condition, so we're looking for eleven-five. Would you be looking to put down a payment today?" Ron asked sizing De'Quan up. To many days, people come into the dealership just to ask a hundred questions and don't buy the car.

"I can do a lot can you open up the door?" De'Quan said ignoring his question.

"Oh yeah, sure", Ron said pulling out the keys. He gave De'Quan the key and let him open the door. He sat down and gripped the steering wheel to feel himself for a moment. Meika popped open the passenger side door and got in. De'Quan ignored her and scanned the dash board.

"Go ahead, start it up", Ron said as he stood in the doorway.

He started the car and it came right on. "Sounds good", Q said as he walked to the front. "Pop the hood Quan".

De'Quan popped the hood and looked at the lit up dash, "53,000 miles on it".

"Yeah, and she handles these city bumps like a champ, trust me, my brother-in-law had one of these. Real nice car", Ron said.

Meika popped open the glove compartment and De'Quan snapped, "Close that, don't touch nothing, I didn't even buy it yet and you already touching shit that don't have nothing to do with you".

"Okay, damn. You don't have to yell", she said as she closed it and sat back in her seat with an attitude.

"Give it some gas", Q said from the front of the car.

De'Quan revved up the engine and couple of times until Q was satisfied. "Looks good, you said it got 50,000 on it".

"Yeah, and it smells like new money up in here son", De'Quan said feeling the excitement slowly creeping up on him. He got out the car and stepped over to Ron as Q sat behind the wheel.

"You said you want eleven-five for this."

"Yes, what does your credit look like?" Ron asked.

"How about I give you ten-five right now for the car? No credit check. Just me giving you the cash, and me driving away".

Ron had to laugh, "You got some balls Mr.?"

"De'Quan Short", he said as they shook hands for the first time.

"You got ten-five right now for this car, than we can do business", Ron said with a bright smile on his face.

De'Quan dug into one of his pocket's and pulled out a nice size brick rubber banded up. "Mr. Ron let's do business my man".

Chapter 26

De'Quan was beginning to feel the power of having your own car after riding around the city for three weeks. Now he felt it was time to flex that power at New York City elite night club The Tunnel. Q sat in the passenger seat with his Yankee hat pulled down low, while Ne'Sean rode in the back.

"Got damn son, look at all the chicks on the line", Ne'Sean beamed over the music playing in the car.

De'Quan rolled the Lexus down 27th street at 5 miles an hour so they could scope out the long line running up the side of the building, and the chicks on the line could see what they were sitting in. You couldn't tell De'Quan he wasn't a part of the New York elite now, and he didn't have to sell any drugs or put out a rap album to do it neither.

"Shit what Flex said, 'first five hundred bitches free'. Let me find a spot, I know that shit is already packed", De'Quan said.

The Tunnel was famous for Funk Master Flex spinning the latest hits every Sunday night. The hostess Mecca promoted the first 500 women free and the club was able to hold 3000 plus party goers, making The Tunnel New York City's grand finale to long party weekends.

Ne'Sean had never been in The Tunnel before, making his first glimpse of the large dance floor when they walked up in the club breath taking. Ne'Sean had been to plenty of house parties in his young years, but never to a club as large as this one. The three of them set up shop on the wall across from the bar and smoked blunt after blunt, soaking in the vibes and action that passed by them like a party train.

"I'm going to the dance floor to get up on some ass", Ne'Sean said as he broke away from his brother and Q.

"A'ight. If you don't see us down here, than check upstairs", Q said over the load sounds of Mic Geronimo's 'I'm so High'.

Ne'Sean nodded his head then disappeared into the flow of the moving line that was headed toward the dance floor.

De'Quan bobbed his head to the music taking slow pulls off of his blunt when his vision was suddenly invaded by one of the baddest sisters he saw pass by him all night. Out of reflex, De'Quan stuck his hand out and gently grabbed her on her wrist. The girl froze, looked at his face real quick, and then stepped out of the moving line. The girl that was directly behind her also stepped off the moving line and by chance she had to occupy the small space that was in front of Q.

De'Quan leaned in close to her ear and said, "I didn't mean to grab you like that, but I could not let you pass me by without saying something".

She looked him up and down and liked red Polo teddy bear sweater and red Yankee hat set up he had going on. The club was to dark in the area for her to see what kind of sneakers he had on.

On the flip side of things, De'Quan was quickly analyzing the cutie he just pulled over. Versace shades, silk jacket, and he got a glimpse of a backside. Nice.

"Ok, so say something", she said snapping him out of his trance.

De'Quan smiled, "You a frisky one huh, my name is De'Quan".

"My name is India".

"Where you from India?" De'Quan asked pulling her closer to him.

"We're from Connecticut".

"Oh yeah, and what made yah come all the way down here on a Sunday night?" De'Quan asked.

"It's my birthday. So I wanted to go where it was live at tonight", India said as she began to move her body to the beat.

"Oh word, you hear that Q, shorty here is a birthday girl", De'Quan said.

Q looked over from India's friend and said, "So I've heard."

De'Quan laughed and said, "You want to make a move to the bathroom".

"That will work", Q said then turned back to India's friend to give her an update.

"We never been here before, what's in the bathroom?" India asked.

De'Quan felt his stock rise to the ceiling. Bad chick - check, from out of town - check. It's her birthday, double check. She's got to be down for anything. De'Quan smiled and said, "Everything, couches, the bar, and more room to breathe".

India looked back at her friend who was all ears in their conversation and nodded her head.

"Lead the way then player", India said as De'Quan took her hand and did just that. He lead the way through the live crowd that danced from the bar all the way up the lit up steps, and down the hallway to The Tunnel's famous unisex bathroom, which had two full bars, couches lining the walls, and big speakers posted up in every corner. The bathroom itself began with a few sinks and mirrors, which lead off like a separate wing with close to thirty stalls in it.

The two couples found an empty couch off to the side next to the bathroom sinks and De'Quan asked her, "What you drinking?"

India smiled, "Whatever you have in mind".

De'Quan laughed and said, "Okay, we'll be back. Come on Q".

When De'Quan and Q walked away, India turned to her friend and said, "Kim what you think girl?"

146

"They cute, you think they getting money?"

"I think they doing something, but it doesn't matter, it's my birthday and I just want to have a good time with some cool guy's".

At the bar, De'Quan and Q each ordered a bottle of Dom P, "what you think?"

Q popped in some tic-tac's and said, "Yo shorty was talking some things. We should try and fuck these chicks in the bathroom".

De'Quan thought about it and smiled, "word son, that way we don't have to pay for a hotel".

They both grabbed a bottle and two glasses and Q said, "Fuck it. Let's bet a buck to see who can fuck first up in here tonight".

They laughed and De'Quan said, "Hell yeah. That's a bet".

✳✳✳✳✳

The Dom P. and conversation flowed until India changed the subject, "I was thinking De'Quan, we should stop playing games and head into the stall, and see what's good for tonight".

De'Quan tried his best to keep a straight face. Her directness caught him off guard, but he kept it smooth and said, "You know, we must have mental telepathy or something, because I was thinking the same thing".

"Or it might be something in this Dom P." India leaned in close to his ear, and purred in a sexy voice and continued, "Whatever it is, it has me extremely hot. Meet me in the last stall in five minutes".

India got up gently took Kim's hand and they disappeared into the stall wing of the bathroom. De'Quan and Q watched them walk away, then they looked at each other and smiled.

"This one might be a tie", De'Quan said.

Q laughed and said, "Fuck it, since you driving, I'll buy the breakfast. Now let's go handle this business".

De'Quan took a last swig of his Dom P. then stepped into the stall area. He walked down the short aisle that ended in a T shape and looked to his right. India was patiently waiting outside the last stall. De'Quan wandered over nonchalantly acting like he also was waiting for a stall to empty out.

Q wandered down to the top of the T and looked to his right. When he saw De'Quan and India waiting down that end, Q turned left figuring that had to be his route to go. Q was drunk but he was on point on what was supposed to go down. He staggered down the aisle not knowing where Kim was waiting at, but the fun and games were all good with him.

De'Quan stood two feet away from India laughing to himself as he watched Q's drunk ass wander down the aisle. He didn't hear the stall behind him open up, but he did catch a glimpse of somebody walk pass him. Before De'Quan could react, he felt a hand grab on his collar and pull him into the stall.

"Oh shit", De'Quan mumbled as India closed the stall door, dug under her skirt and pulled off her panties without any hesitation.

"Oh shit", De'Quan blurted out again as he stood frozen in the stall.

India moved in close and said, "You can't believe this is happening...can you".

Without waiting for his answer, India took charge and began to undo his belt and zipper. De'Quan quickly snapped out of it and pulled out his condom. India turned around put one foot on the toilet bowl, and one hand on the stall door. She put her other hand on the connecting stalls wall and arched her back.

De'Quan stood back and watched her ass cheeks spread open like they had a mind of their own.

In the background, De'Quan heard the d.j. put on Mobb Deep's Shook Ones part2 as he was entering India from the back. The club erupted in a load roar like they were cheering him on. In his mind, De'Quan was doing this for all of mankind and he had to represent as he rocked to India's rhythm, while she bounced to Shook Ones part2.

India was in a zone as she stroked De'Quan's over excited ego with her moaning and dirty talk, "Ooooh, get this pussy nigga. Ooooh, get this pussy nigga".

Then he felt it. The point when he knew he should have pulled out of her, but he was at the point of no return, and it felt so good, De'Quan couldn't stop himself. Just a few more seconds and it will be over. They both began to climax at the same time, with India almost pulling down the stall connecting wall. De'Quan's knees buckled and he almost lost his balance.

De'Quan put his back against the wall to catch his breath, as India's shoe slipped on the toilet and she stepped inside of it with a big splash. "Shit".

As much as De'Quan wanted to laugh, his mind was somewhere else. They gave each other as much space as they could in the small stall and De'Quan gave her his back. He looked down at his dick and he was right about the feeling he felt. The condom broke.

He dropped the rest of the condom in the toilet and flushed it, and then he fixed his pants. When De'Quan turned around India was gone. At first, he thought he just had a good ass dream, but then her scent rose up off of his sweater. It was real, but where did she go so fast he asked himself as he stepped out in the T shape corridor and bumped into a girl who looked like she was on the verge of throwing up. She pushed pass De'Quan and quickly shut the door behind herself.

De'Quan walked down to the other side of the T, "Yo Q".

When De'Quan didn't get an answer he walked down to the last stall and saw that the door was half open. He pushed it open and was shocked to see Q sitting on the toilet with his pants down to his ankles, passed out.

"Shit, Yo Q, get the fuck up son. Aww man this shit is crazy", De'Quan said smacking Q hard enough to wake him up.

"What the fuck man!"

"Man, pull your damn pants up so we can get out of here. Look at you man, I wish I had a camera", De'Quan said as he backed out of the stall and started laughing.

Q closed the stall and got himself together. The toilet flushed and Q emerged feeling disorientated, "Fuck is so funny".

De'Quan lit up a cigarette and said, "You might owe me a hundred dollars, that's what".

"How you figure that?"

"Because I bet you don't even remember if you fucked shorty or not", De'Quan said.

Q looked around to make sure nobody was listening to their exchange and said, "I fucked her. Why else would my pants be down like that".

"Because she fucked you!" De'Quan said and they burst out laughing. "Yo let's go find Ne'Sean and get up out of here".

Chapter 27

"Hello?"

"What's up Meika, its Dre. Is your brother there?"

"No, but Ne'Sean is here. You want to talk to him?"

"Yeah", Dre said and waited for him to come on the other line.

"Hello".

"What's the deal Dunn", Dre said.

"Yo what up Dre, how you doing in there?" Ne'Sean said.

Dre shifted in his seat and said, "Ain't nothing, just holding shit down. What's up with Quan?"

"Oh he went away for a few days to go see Pop up in Clinton. You know he copped a Lexus, so that nigga been all over the place. I didn't even see him before he left".

"Damn, he didn't leave anything for me?" Dre asked.

Ne'Sean thought about it for a second, then said, "Nah, not that I know of. Like I said, I didn't see him before he left. Why you need some money or something?"

"Nah, I need you to make a run for me to this chick crib in Brownsville. She's waiting for Quan to bring it to her, but since he's gone I need you to give it to her".

"What you want me to bring her?" Ne'Sean asked as he grabbed a pen and paper.

"I need like ten body bags from Lewis, you feel me?" Dre said hoping he wouldn't have to break it all down to Ne'Sean over the phone.

Ne'Sean went into his room and went into his brother money stash. "Okay. I got some dough out of Quan's stash. Give me her number and address and I'll take it to her tonight".

Dre breathed a sigh of relief and gave him the info. When he hung up the phone, Dre walked to the back of the dorm and sat down on his bunk. Since he's been on the end side things had been going smooth for Dre. He had one fight his first day in the dorm for phone time. Once some of the other Brooklyn boys saw Dre could hold his own they welcome him with open arms and he hasn't had any problems since.

Dre stayed in contact with De'Quan whenever he could catch him in the house and he kept Dre up on what was going on in the hood. The gossip was cool with Dre but lately he had been feeling like they needed to do more with their lives. They had a nice stash of dough in Rahkem's house and Dre kept his separate stash with Tammy. Nobody wanted to leave any money in Dre's house without him being there, so Dre wasn't surprised to hear De'Quan brought a car. The last hit they did gave them a lot of breathing room to buy things they wouldn't normally buy. Dre knew if he was home he would done the same thing. Sitting in jail had him thinking they had to change that way of thinking or else they're going to be robbing drug dealers until they're old and grey.

Tammy stuck to her word and came through to see him no less than two days a week. Those hour visits were tough on the both of them at first, but once Dre got himself situated in the dorm he was able to focus more on their relationship and how far they could go if he came home with good plan.

"Yo what's good kid, what you thinking about?" Black Cee asked Dre snapping him out of his trance.

"What I'm going to do when I get out of here. Can't think about nothing else", Dre said.

"Soon as we smoke that next batch your mind is going to be somewhere else", Black Cee said and handed Dre a cigarette. "Here, bust me down".

"Yeah I just called my man and he wasn't there, but I got his brother to drop it off to her. So make sure Macho calls her, cause they going over there tonight".

"Okay, how much they giving her?" Black Cee asked.

"Ten 20bags from Lewis", Dre said in-between pulls of the cigarette.

"Okay, I'm on him", Black Cee said as he stood up, took the half of cigarette from Dre and walked off to go handle his business.

That's why Dre liked Black Cee; he was all about his business. Dre could tell all Black Cee did in the streets was hustle. The first night Dre was in the dorm he beat a kid up in the bathroom for some phone time and Black Cee was the first one to pull Dre to the side and told him how the Brooklyn boys stuck together in there. Dre didn't want any free rides so he told Black Cee he came in with some dope and weed on him and he wanted to sell some to get some food and other necessities before they went to commissary. Black Cee hustled off all the dope and they smoked the weed, and they've been partners ever since.

Black Cee found Macho; whose girl was willing to bring in more drugs for him, and Dre had De'Quan drop the drugs off at Macho's girl house. Everything was going smooth until De'Quan brought the car and stopped coming home as much to catch his calls. Catching Ne'Sean in the house and getting him to make the run for him was the shot in the arm they needed, because they ran out of weed two weeks ago and Macho was short to go home. So getting a big package will be just what the doctor ordered to hold them down for a little while.

$$*****$$

When Ne'Sean hung up the phone with Dre, he called Jamel and asked him to make a run with him. Jamel was sitting in the house bored out of his mind, so he didn't have to ask him twice. Ne'Sean got dress and put on one of his brother leather jackets. He went into one of the Nike boxes and took one of De'Quan 9mm's and tucked it in his inside jacket pocket. Ne'Sean usually didn't like carrying guns, but he was no fool. Brownsville is a very harsh place at night.

Ne'Sean met Jamel downstairs and the hailed a cab. On their way to Lewis and Halsey to pick up the weed, Jamel pestered Ne'Sean the whole time about the trip being more than a business run for his brother while he was gone.

"Is she going to have any friends over there?"

"Jamel I don't even know what the chick looks like", Ne'Sean said sounding uninterested.

"That don't mean she's not going to have any friends over there", Jamel said. He knew only good things could happen to them for stepping in for De'Quan.

"From what Dre told me shorty got a man or some shit like that", Ne'Sean said as he stared out the window.

"Jamel's face lit up, "Where, in jail with Dre? Aww man, that's even better. Her man is locked up and she's horny, don't you see".

Wondering what the hell made him bring Jamel on this mission, Ne'Sean said, "No, I don't see. Look we're in and out of there. I don't like being around them Brownsville niggas. Them niggas steal sneakers off of dead people feet".

Jamel laughed and said, "You ain't lying about that, but don't be surprised if we walk in there and there's three Goddesses in there ready to get busy".

154

"Yeah I hear you", Ne'Sean said before he hopped out the cab to go grab the weed.

When they pulled up in front of 312 Saratoga Ne'Sean tried to get the cab driver to wait for them.

"Sorry boss, I'm not waiting for my mother out here longer than a New York minute. That will be 15dollars please", the cab driver said ready to get out of dodge.

Once Ne'Sean knew it was a lost cause he paid the man and they made their way to the building. As they walked past the late night stares and glares from the people hanging out in the front, Jamel thought he saw saliva dripping from the corners of a few of the guys mouths. Jamel tried to keep his vision straight as he followed Ne'Sean into the building.

When they got on the elevator, Jamel said, "Damn Sean, them niggas looked thirsty as hell out there".

"Don't worry; I got one of Quan's biscuits on me. So you don't have to tuck in your spaghetti chain", Ne 'Sean joked.

"Real funny", Jamel said as the elevator door popped open and they walked to the apartment door. Ne'Sean knocked on the door and the music that was playing inside turned down a little.

"Who is it?"

"Ne'Sean, is Ebony home?"

The door was opened and Ebony looked surprised to see two people standing at her door, "Who is this?"

Ne'Sean stared at her for a second was taken aback by her beauty. Ebony's hair was pinned up in a dobe style, which brought out her smooth facial features. Ebony stood behind the door only revealing her face looking from Ne'Sean to Jamel.

"Oh, this is my friend Jamel".

Jamel put on his winning smile and waved to her. She looked him up and down then opens the door wider to let them in, "Sit on the couch".

When they sat on the couch, they were able to see what Ebony was wearing and it made both of their hearts skip a beat. Ebony was wearing a red silk Victoria Secret robe that was only thigh high and revealed more then she was supposed to be showing at the moment. The boys sat there stuck.

Ebony was thick for her 5'2 frame and whenever she walked, it looked like the robe was threatening to show more of her ass with every step she took. "So you got that?"

Ne'Sean snapped out of the trance she had them in and said, "Aww yeah".

"Come put it on the table", Ebony ordered as she sat at the dining table.

Ne'Sean dumped the ten bags on the table and he was caught by her powerful scent. It smelled intoxicating.

"You smoke?" She asked Ne'Sean.

"Nah".

"What about your friend?" She asked and they both looked over to Jamel. He quickly nodded his head.

Ebony walked over to the stereo and grabbed a bag of weed and philly blunt off the top of it. Her walk from the stereo over to Jamel was so seductive he caught himself catching a minor hard on.

"Here, roll this up", Ebony ordered handing it to Jamel.

Ne'Sean wasn't feel the direction this simple drop off was going, so he tried to stop it, "Ebony we need to call a cab, if that's okay with you".

Jamel snapped at Ne'Sean, "Damn Sean what's the rush. After this blunt we can call a cab".

Ebony walked over to Ne'Sean and touched his chest, "Yeah Ne'Sean, what's the rush? It's only 9:30, I know you don't have to run home this early".

Ne'Sean's heart felt like it was about to explode out of his chest. She was making him high off of her scent and the closer she moved in the more nervous he got. He looked over to Jamel, who looked like he didn't know whether to roll the blunt or watch them. Ebony slowly licked the side of Ne'Sean's ear. At that moment, Jamel knew it was going down; he ripped the wrapper off of the philly and went to work on the blunt.

Ne'Sean blushed and said, "Aww, can I have some juice?"

"Sure baby", Ebony said in the sexiest voice Ne'Sean ever heard and strutted into the kitchen.

Ne'Sean got up and went over to the couch. The nervous look on his face told on him before he could say it, "Yo man, did you see what she did to me?"

Jamel was all smiles, "I told you it was going down tonight, just chill man".

Ebony came out of the kitchen with two glasses of red kool-aid and gave it to them. She turned the music up a notch and sat on the couch in-between them. She gave Jamel the lighter and they sat there smoking until Ne'Sean was nice off the contact. Feeling good Ebony got up and started dancing in front of them. She could tell from the look on Jamel's face he wasn't leaving no matter what. Ne'Sean still looked confused about what was happening.

Ebony reached out and took Ne'Sean's hand, pulling him off of the couch, "Dance with me".

The dancing turned to grinding in the middle of the livingroom floor, while Jamel drooled on himself watching the show. Ebony stuck her down Ne'Sean's pants and grabbed on his penis like she owned it. He opened up her robe and started playing with her coco brown 36c's knowing there was no turning back now.

She undid his pants and started sucking on his penis as Jamel watched in shock. Ne'Sean was totally lost in the moment as he fucked her face like they were the only people in the room. When he came Ebony swallowed every drop causing Ne'Sean's knees to buckle.

"Oh shit", He fell to the floor tangled up in his own pants from not taking them off and stared at Ebony as she moved on to Jamel like a professional porn star.

Jamel was so excited he almost came in his pants before she even touched him. Ebony went in a small drawer and pulled out a condom. "Pull your pants down", she told Jamel, who wasted no time undoing his belt and pants. She put the condom on him, pulled her panties off and took Jamel on the ride of his life until they both climaxed.

"You can call that cab now", Ebony said before walking off to the bathroom, leaving Ne'Sean and Jamel stunned and spent in her livingroom.

✱✱✱✱✱

Ne'Sean and Jamel waited for the elevator in silence, lost in his own thoughts about what just happen. When they stepped onto the elevator, Jamel broke the silence, "Now that session was official!"

They started laughing and Ne'Sean said, "Yo don't tell De'Quan what happen up there. He's going to flip if he finds out we did the drop instead of him, and Ebony turned out to be cold freak".

"What, are you serious? You think Quan ain't fuck that chick too? She's a freak son, I know De'Quan hit that", Jamel said feeling confident about what he was saying. The elevator stopped on the first floor and Jamel pushed the outer door open to walk out first. When he stepped out into the lobby, a hand suddenly reached out and snatched his chain.

"Oh shit!" Jamel blurted out as he fell back into Ne'Sean, and they fell back into the elevator. Ne'Sean stepped back and pulled out the 9mm as they both rushed back off of the elevator and watched the tail end of the chain snatcher running up the stairs.

"That motherfucker snatched my shit!"

Jamel flinched like he was going to run after him, but Ne'Sean quickly grabbed his arm, "Nah son, fuck that shit. Let's get the fuck out of here".

"What…That nigga got my shit!" Jamel said fuming from the incident.

"Man that shit ain't worth it and this might be a set up. Let's get the fuck out of this neighborhood", Ne'Sean said. He looked out the front window of the building and saw the cab sitting by the curb with the engine running.

Ne'Sean put the gun back inside his coat and they walked out of the building past the same group that was out there when they came in. Jamel open the cab door and hopped in while Ne'Sean watched his back.

"Nostrand and Park", Ne'Sean told the driver as he stuffed a twenty dollar bill through the bullet proof partition.

When the driver pulled away from the curb, a shot rang out causing Ne'Sean and Jamel to duck, and cab driver to step on the gas pedal. The crowd in front of the building shared a laugh as they watched the cab screech around the corner and out of sight.

Chapter 28

Dre being locked up gave De'Quan a lot of solo time to drive around and think about how his life is supposed to go moving forward. De'Quan had been spending more time than he wanted with Shakia, so getting a car was a good move for him. Shakia was crazy, sexy, and cool all wrapped into a nice package they both knew De'Quan couldn't unwrap, because he was Dre best friend and she his sister. The attraction was there, but the reality of the situation as a whole wasn't. Once De'Quan got the car he kept Shakia at arms distance with a million excuses of places to go and people to see, until he took the long drive to go see Pop.

A lot has changed for De'Quan since Pop went to prison, and not being able to talk to him about it was killing him. Pop was moved to Clinton Correctional Facility, a one hundred year old maximum security prison 20 minutes from the Canadian border to the north, and seven hours from New York City. Making the trip by himself would be good for the both of them, De'Quan was pretty sure Pop had a lot to discuss with him, and having Mama K, Ne'Sean and Meika on the visit would not work out right.

De'Quan pulled into the closest town to the prison and grabbed a room in a motel 6 to get some rest. The next morning he drove over to Clinton got processed, and was on the visit floor by 10:15 a.m.

During a week day, the visit room would be light when it came to activity, with the heavier traffic coming in on the weekends. De'Quan made a Tuesday his first visit day, and he planned on staying in the motel 6 for the rest of the week.

De'Quan had to check in with one of the ugliest women he had ever seen at the c.o. desk on the visiting floor, and he was seated at a table close to a window by another officer. De'Quan brought a few things out of the vending machines, and it turned out the wait for Pop to come out took longer than the actual processing De'Quan went through to get in. Hunger took over and De'Quan ended up eating half the food before Pop could check in at the same c.o. desk he had too. When he strolled over to where his son was waiting for him, Pop's face lit up.

"Damn boy, you're almost bigger than me now", Pop said as the hugged and sat down. Pop looked at the garbage on the table and said, "And I see you ate up everything already".

De'Quan smiled, "Man, I was starving Pop, what you want from the machines?"

Pop looked at a few things that were still untouched and grabbed a cheese Danish. "I'm good with this for now, so how was your drive?"

"How did you know I drove here?' De'Quan asked looking puzzled.

Pop laughed and said, "I called your mother the other day, but she didn't tell me you was coming".

"Pop I have something for you", De'Quan said as he shifted in his seat.

Pop didn't expect anything from his son but good news and a good laugh, "What you got?"

"I got some Lewis and Halsey in one thing, and some Hancock and Evergreen in the other. You can mix it up if you want, but trust me, they're both banging separately", De'Quan said with a sly smile on his face.

Pop didn't like what he was hearing.

"Look, you didn't have to bring me none of that. The last thing I need is for you to get into trouble over some petty shit".

De'Quan knew Pop was going to beef with him about bringing him the weed, but he wanted to show Pop he was all grown up now. "Pop I know, but I got this, don't worry about it".

Pop shifted in his seat. The boy is hard headed like somebody he knows. "Alright, don't be doing this shit all the time; these crackers are crazy up here. Go to the machines and heat me up two fish and cheese sandwiches. Put them things in a bag of chips over there while you wait. And watch the fat chick, she's miserable and likes to fuck with people".

De'Quan did what Pop told him to do and when he returned to the table Pop sent him back to the machine for a bottle of water. While the c.o.'s sitting at the desk watched De'Quan and the rest of the visitors at the machines, Pop stuffed the two balloons of weed in his drawers.

When De'Quan finally sat down, they got into a long conversation about the house, and what was happening in the store on a daily basis. Pop sat there and listened to his son, thinking of a good time to ask him about his dealings in the streets. Many nights, he laid up in a cell and thought about the path his oldest son was on.

"De'Quan I need you to be straight with me okay", Pop said once he felt they were comfortable.

De'Quan shook his head yes. He knew it was coming. No matter how many times he went over it in his mind about what he was going to say to his father when the time came, he still didn't know how he was going to tell him what he has been doing in his absence.

"I've been investigating you and your friend's for a while now, and the only thing I know for sure is yah are not selling any drugs in Marcy. Which is a good thing, but people don't just buy G.S.300's out of nowhere without having a job. So fill me in Quan.

"Remember, you're my son, and I understand more than you probably think, but don't lie to me. Now start from the top", Pop said looking his son straight in the eyes.

De'Quan took a deep breath and said, "Pop when you got knocked, I knew I was the man of the house. I didn't want us to have to ask nobody in that projects for nothing. Me and Dre talked about it and we knew we didn't want to sell drugs. It takes up too much time and everybody is in your business.

"I found one of your guns and we used it to rob a bodega", De'Quan said and watched Pop's reaction before he continued.

Pop did not want to show too much emotion until he heard all of his son sins, but he had to flinch when De'Quan said they had been out doing robberies. He thought they were selling drugs in another projects or boro.

"We did a couple of places, brought more guns, and saved up most of the money. Then Grand-Ma Trina's house caught fire, we didn't even know it was money in there. So we did a big hit and gave Mama K the money for the store and we still had something left over", De'Quan said.

"So now that Dre is in jail, what are you doing?" Pop asked.

"I haven't done anything. I can't see myself moving without Dre Pop. I know he got my back and I got his", De'Quan said confidently.

Pop let it all soak in then asked, "Is your brother running around with yah?"

De'Quan knew Pop was going to ask him that, and he also knew Pop would not swallow Ne'Sean being in the streets with him and his friends. He told himself on the drive up there he will have to lie about Ne'Sean's involvement.

"Nah Pop, Ne'Sean is about to go to college and all that soon. There's no way we want him running with us".

"Okay, so now that you have all of this free time on your hands, why haven't you gone to a trade school or something like Mama K asked? These streets aren't promised to anyone as you can see".

"I know Pop…I mean I heard Mama K, but it's like…"

De'Quan stopped in mid-sentence and Pop could see his son was struggling with his inner demons. "I know it is hard son to hold down the family while I'm in here, and living in Brooklyn makes things worst. See son we come from a world where the Real Always Wins.

"You come from a winning blood line, but the times have changed, and the hood is changing right before our eyes. We have to change with it. You already have the vision because you knew it wasn't good timing to go out into the projects and sell drugs after I got locked up for it.

"But I expect you to spend that Real energy you have on something that has a better future for the family, than the one I choose", Pop said as De'Quan hung on his every word.

Pop was always a good teacher to his children and all of the reading he was doing in prison made him feel like he had so much to give them now from it. "Are you driving back home today?"

"Nah, I'm going to stay up here for a few days", De'Quan said looking at the clock.

"Okay good. Then I guess that's enough preaching for today. The visit is over in ten minutes anyway", Pop said.

They talked until the c.o. at the desk stood up and said, "Alight...Visits are over".

Pop shook his head and said, "What I tell you, she's miserable, I'll see you tomorrow son".

"Cool Pop", De'Quan laughed as they hugged and Pop went back through the thick steel gates.

Chapter 29

With De'Quan being out of town, Rahkem was feeling a burst of energy to go out and splurge a little with De'Quan and company money. The way Rahkem was seeing it, De'Quan just brought a car before he left, so he won't miss a few hundred dollars.

Rahkem stepped out on Fulton Street and brought himself a new Polo outfit, and a pair of Reebox. Once he went home to change, Rahkem took a cab over to Patchen and Quincy to pick up a honey complexion sister named Diamond. Rahkem was feeling lucky tonight, and if his luck was right he might get some Kat from Diamond, or even her real name before the night is over.

Diamond came downstairs did up in a Banana Republic jean suit that hugged every curve God blessed her with. Rahkem broke out in a sweat just watching her walk over to the cab. They went downtown to 44th street to Beefsteak Charlie's, got down on plates of the chicken and shrimp combo, and sipped on long Island ice teas. The conversation flowed and they laughed at each other's jokes like they really enjoyed each other's company.

After diner, they went down to 42nd street to see the new hip-hop movie out called 'The Show'. She was feeling it, he wasn't.

All of this pampering gave Rahkem a reason to get bold on her when they got in the cab and dictate the next destination. "We are going to Marcy and Flushing".

Diamond sat back without protesting. If he wanted to go to his house instead of hers, than that was fine with her. Diamond had it on her mind to see where Rahkem lived at anyway, since he was talking all this Willy stuff to her like he making some real money.

As they got off of the elevator on Rahkem's floor, they see his brother Tye backing out of the house with a small book bag in his hand. "What's up Tye, what you doing here?"

Rahkem's voice startled Tye, he turned around and slowly put on his vote for me smile and said, "well, well, well who you have here lil bro?"

Feeling good, smelling good, and now his brother was bigging him up for the piece he just brought home. Rahkem knew this was his night. He smiled and said, "This here is Diamond. Diamond this is my brother Tye".

Five seconds of awkward silence filled the hallway as Diamond smiled at Tye, and Tye thought about his getaway.

"What's in the bag Tye?" Rahkem asked after staring at the bag.

For a moment, Tye felt like a cornered cat, and then the thought hit him. Rahkem can't beat him. Tye looked from his brother over to Diamond, licked his lips and said, "I came to pick something up, why?"

Rahkem began to feel queasy inside as bells started going off in his head. "What you came to pick up?"

"None of your business", Tye blasted as his muscles tensed up.

Rahkem and Diamond stood there frozen as Tye tried to push pass them and get to the elevator. Rahkem knew what was in the bag. He just didn't know how much and he wasn't trying to find out later. Rahkem reached out and tried to snatch the bag out of Tye's hand. Anticipating his little brother might try something stupid; Tye pulled the bag back and hit Rahkem with a left hook to his jaw.

"What the fuck you doing?"

Rahkem crumbed to the floor. "What you do that for?" Rahkem cried out as Diamond jumped back saying, "Oh shit".

Tye told himself fuck the elevator and made his getaway to the stairs. Diamond reached down to Rahkem to help him up, "Oh my God, are you alright?"

Disgusted with himself for letting his brother play him like that, Rahkem let her help him up and he quickly dusted himself off. He made a dash for the stairs and took them two at a time down to the lobby. By the time Rahkem made out the front of the building the only people walking around were crack heads and the project night life. Rahkem didn't know what to do. He walked back into the building and the elevator suddenly open to ruin the rest of his night.

Diamond stepped off the elevator and said, "Aww, I'm sorry Rahkem, but I gots to go".

Rahkem touched his soar jaw and said, "Hold on Diamond that was about nothing. Me and my brother fight all the time".

"That's good and all, but I'm still going home", Diamond said with her mind made up already.

"Come up stairs, and I can call you a cab", Rahkem said, trying one last push to keep her with him.

Diamond bushed him off and made her way through the front door, "Nah that's okay, I'll catch a cab on the ave. Call me sometime".

"Shit!"

From the lobby all the way up to his room all Rahkem could think about is damage control. When he got into his room, he ran straight to where he had the money stashed at. Tye took everything. Damage control quickly turned into Rahkem sitting on the edge of his bed, putting his face in his hands and crying.

*****

The next day Ne'Sean and Jamel were in the park sitting on the benches with their girl friends when a distraught looking Rahkem came into the park.

"Hey what's up yah…Ne'Sean can I talk to you for a minute?"

Karman looked from Rahkem to Ne'Sean, and he smiled at her, "It's okay baby". Ne'Sean kissed her and said, "I'll be right back".

When they were out of ear shot Rahkem said, "My brother did it".

Ne'Sean was already bored with this story. Rahkem's jaw was swollen and the way Ne'Sean saw it everybody fight's with their older brother. "So what do you want with me?"

Rahkem shifted in his stance, he just got there and he was already losing his audience, he swallowed hard and said, "Listen man, I don't know how Quan is going to take this, but my brother took the money".

"He did what? Where the fuck is he?" Ne'Sean barked, clearly upset about the news.

"I don't know, I've been looking for that nigga all night and all day, today", Rahkem whined.

"You know you done fucked up right", Ne'Sean said ready to bust Rahkem upside his head.

"Ne'Sean please talk to your brother and them for me, I'm sorry this happen man, I swear", Rahkem said right to break down aging.

Just for him begging Ne'Sean lost his cool and smacked him on the other side of his face. "What you do that for?"

Ne'Sean was furious with how soft Rahkem was, "Man snap out of it. You standing up here crying like some bitch. Just be cool. When De'Quan comes back we'll fix this, now where does your brother live at?"

Rahkem told him and Ne'Sean said, "Aight take your ass home and wait for us to call you". Rahkem nodded his head like an obedient dog and ran off with his tail between his legs.

Ne'Sean went back over to the benches and kissed Karman, "What happen baby?"

"I have to go take care of some business for my brother", Ne'Sean said not wanting to say too much. Ne'Sean liked Karman a lot but she didn't know about how they got their money.

"But I thought we were going upstairs for a little while today?" Karman asked with her bottom lip poking out. She pulled him close to her and started kissing on his ear. Karman's heavy breathing caused Ne'Sean to get a small tingle in his pants, and he knew he had to control himself for now.

"I'll try and be back in an hour, okay".

Karman batted her eyes and said, "Okay, but if you not coming back, you better call me".

He smiled and said, "Okay, yo Jamel we got to bounce".

Jamel looked up from kissing his girl friend on her neck, with a lost look in his eyes and said, "What, I thought we were going to slide upstairs".

"Yeah, but something came up. Sorry about this Sky, but we'll be back". Ne'Sean said and led the way out of the park while Jamel reluctantly followed.

On the walk to his house, Ne'Sean filled Jamel in on what happened and what he planned on doing about it. Jamel wanted to go back to the benches and finish what he started with Sky, but Ne'Sean was his brother from another mother and no matter crazy Ne'Sean's plans sound to him, Jamel had to go hold him down.

"Here put this on", Ne'Sean said handing Jamel a black hoody.

Jamel took the hoody and started getting second thought's, "Yo man, I don't know why we can't just wait until De'Quan comes back. He'll…"

"Check it Jamel, you my dawg right?" Ne'Sean snapped at him.

"Yeah, but I…"

"Then stop crying about it. I know what I'm doing, and I want to catch this nigga before he spends all the dough". Ne'Sean went underneath the bed and pulled out a Timberland box with four guns in it and a few boxes of bullets as he continued with his rant.

"We'll be in and out of there. You think I want to have a conversation with this nigga, I just want our dough back, that's it".

Ne'Sean loaded up two 9mm's and he handed one to Jamel. He took a $140 out the box for himself and he gave Jamel $60. "What's this for?"

Ne'Sean rolled his eyes, "Just in case we get separated, duuhhh. Now you got dough to get back to the crib. Now let's go".

On their way to Nostrand Avenue to catch a cab, Ne'Sean saw a crack head he knew had a car. "What's up Dornell, what you doing right now?"

Dornell scratched his dirty beard and said, "I ain't doing shit, why, what's up little nigga?"

"You still got a car?"

"Yeah, why you want to go somewhere?" Dornell asked licking his lips. He hadn't had a hit all day and he knew these kids didn't sell drugs, which meant they could pay him in cash, even better.

"Let us hold your car for an hour, and I'll hit you with $30 dollars", Ne'Sean said.

"Aww man Ne'Sean, I can't give your little ass my car. Yah little niggas will probably wrap my shit around a stop sign. I can drive you though", Dornell said.

Ne'Sean thought to himself 'it was worth a try', he didn't a drivers license anyway. "Aight…but you only getting twenty now".

Dornell didn't care; as long as he had twenty dollars in his pocket when they were done, he was good. "Okay, let's go".

Dornell had a four door 84 Buick that had ashes, empty soda cans, and old food wrappers all over the place. Ne'Sean and Jamel kicked some of the garbage out into the street before hopping in.

Dornell pulled from the curb with a little screech and Jamel found himself sitting in the backseat counting the cigarette burns on the seat. "Damn Dornell, why don't you clean this piece of shit up some time", Jamel said breaking the silence.

"Word son, what do you be thinking about, turn left here", Ne'Sean said as he kept his eyes on the road.

Dornell navigated to the left and said, "Man why you got to talk about my wheels like that. She gets me where I need to go with no problems".

"Well if you keep using her as a garbage can she going to go on strike on your ass on a cold winter night", Jamel said sparking a round of laughs from Ne'Sean and Dornell.

"Pull over here", Ne'Sean said pointing to a parking space. Dornell pulled over to the side and Ne'Sean said, "Wait right here. You leave and you won't get a bonus".

"Why would I leave without my money anyway?" Dornell asked, but his question was ignored as his passengers got out and walked around the corner out of sight.

Tye lived on St. James in a ten family tenement building. The small lobby door locks were broken so they walked right in. "How do you know where you going?" Jamel asked.

Ne'Sean looked over his shoulder as they walked up the stairs and said, "His brother told me stupid, now keep your voice down".

"Why they don't have an elevator in here?" Jamel mumbled to himself as he followed his friend up to the fourth floor.

The dark color walls made the lights on the landing feel dimmer than they were. Ne'Sean walked over to apartment 4a and put his ear to it. Jamel sucked his teeth and said, "What's with the private eyes shit man, just knock on the door".

Ne'Sean gave him the evil eye and pulled out his gun. "Okay smart ass".

He knocked on the door and heard nothing but the sounds of people in the other apartments. After knocking three more times, Ne'Sean gave up and was ready to leave when someone came up the dimly lit staircase. Ne'Sean and Jamel froze as the figure stopped on the landing below and stared up at the two hooded teens.

Ne'Sean couldn't see his face, so he took a shot in the dark and said, "What's up Tye?"

Tye dropped the bag of groceries he was carrying and reached in his waist band for his recently purchased 38 revolver.

"Oh shit!" Jamel blurted out as he tried to scramble in the small hallway.

Ne'Sean already had his gun in his hand, but he didn't anticipate having to use it in a split second situation. He raised it and let off a shot out of fear as he scrambled in the direction Jamel did.

"Shit...little fuck", Tye snarled as he let off three shots in their direction. The gun fire were deafening on the staircase as sounds of panic could be heard coming from the surrounding apartments.

"They shooting! They shooting! Get down...get down!"

"Aww", Jamel cried out as he fell on the stairs. Feeling the heat Ne'Sean turned around and let off four shots at Tye. Tye quickly turned on his heels and dipped down the stairs two at a time.

Ne'Sean turn to Jamel who was gripping his ankle, "Damn son what happen?"

"Shit man, I think I broke my ankle", Jamel said with a pained look on his face.

"Come on son, we have to get out of here, can you walk?" Ne'Sean asked as he helped him up.

"I'm a try", Jamel said, and they began to work their way down the stairs. When they reached the first floor Ne'Sean put his gun in his hand as Jamel held onto his shoulder. He limped out the front door and Tye was nowhere in sight. The faint sounds of a siren sound like it was making its way over into their direction.

"Come on man we got to breeze", Ne'Sean said as Jamel put a pep in his step. When they got to the car Dornell saw the gun in Ne'Sean's hand and almost peed on himself.

"Aww man, what's going on? What happened to him?"

Ne'Sean helped Jamel in the car and quickly hopped in, "Man just drive this motherfucker".

Dornell started up the car and quickly pulled out of the spot, "Where too man", he asked with a nervous look on his face.

"Jamel you think you need to go to a hospital?" Ne'Sean asked not knowing what to do.

"Nah man, let's just go to the crib and put it in ice," Jamel said still holding onto his ankle.

"Cool, take us back to the projects", Ne'Sean ordered trying to calm down.

Dornell kept looking in his rear view mirror like they were being followed, "good man, cause I didn't sign up for all the guns and shit".

Chapter 30

De'Quan had a lot on his mind and it was time to share it with his childhood friend. He called Tammy to see if she was going to see Dre on Rikers Island on a night visit. Tammy said she wasn't feeling well so she was skipping this week night visit. To talk to Dre, De'Quan needed some alone time and Tammy taking a sick day from going to visit Dre is just what De'Quan needed.

After going through the long ordeal of being warned of bringing in contraband and being searched, De'Quan took a seat in a noisy waiting area until he heard Dre's name. He was shuffled into the visiting room and given a table to sit at. Ten minutes later Dre came bouncing out of a sliding door wearing a grey jumpsuit and a pair of Fila slippers. He got close to the table De'Quan stood up and they gave each other a pound and hug.

"What's good man?" Dre said beaming from ear to ear. He hadn't seen De'Quan since the day he came in.

"Ain't nothing, what's good with you?" De'Quan asked as they sat down.

"I'm chilling man. I was expecting Tam to be out here. She didn't come with you?" Dre asked as he scanned the visiting room half expecting to see Tammy pop up.

"She said she wasn't feeling good today. So I gave her the day off", De'Quan joked.

"Oh ok. So what's up?"

"We had to beat up Rahkem", De'Quan said changing is smile into a frown.

"I'm figuring he had it coming for some reason", Dre said bracing himself for a bomb he knew his friend was about to drop on him.

"Fat Pee got more enjoyment out of that than I did", De'Quan said replaying the scene in his head.

"So why yah did it?"

"This motherfucker Rah brother smacked him up and took our money from him", De'Quan said.

Dre's back got straight as a razor, "hold up, what you mean he took our money. How the fuck did he know it was up there?" Dre asked ready to explode.

"That fucking dummy showed it to him", De'Quan said.

They sat there in silence for a few moments, both of them lost in their own thoughts about the lost they took. "What we going to do now?"

"When I spoke to Fat Pee he wanted to bring in Q to take your place, but I don't trust that. Q is good people, but he might freeze up on me and I'm not trying to chance it. We can wait until you come home to do something. By that time I should have a proper spot for us to hit", De'Quan said.

"Damn son, I want to fuck that nigga up right now. Where's Tye at?" Dre asked like he could go looking for him.

"We have no idea. I was up top visiting Pop for a few days when it happen. Ne'Sean and Jamel took it upon themselves to go to Tye house and they got into a shoot out with him. Jamel damn near broke his ankle trying to run. Now the nigga Tye is MIA", De'Quan said shaking his head.

"Damn, we got to smash that nigga", Dre said.

"I know this already, but the bottom line is Tye is gone and we probably won't see him again unless it's his funeral, cause the Tye got mad niggas looking for him", De'Quan said.

"Damn son, I got like a month and a half to come home, and when I touch down I wanted to chill. I didn't want to come home and have to kick in a nigga door", Dre said rubbing his head as if he suddenly got a headache.

"I wanted to chill too. I had a few days to build with Pop and he was telling me about some good money moves we could do and now all that shit is pipe dream".

"Yo I can't believe this shit, what's up with Pop anyway?" Dre asked trying to get off the bad thought's running through his mind. Just yesterday, he had a plan for when he came home, now it was slowly flushing itself down the toilet.

*****

Two weeks later Dre found himself sitting on his bunk staring at his surroundings, Black Cee was being released in a few hours and once he left the dorm would be Dre's to run. Dre was going home in fifteen days; he did not feel like running a jail dorm.

Black Cee came out of the shower room half dressed and ready to roll. He looked at Dre and snapped him out of his trance, "Dre what's up?"

"Ain't nothing, I was just wondering what my girl was doing right now", Dre said.

Black Cee smiled as he put on his sneakers, "Well in two weeks you won't have to worry about that any more".

"Yeah, you right. Plus I was thinking about who might step up now that you bouncing", Dre said.

Black Cee glanced over the dorm room and said, "Well Lite and them are from the Fort and they starting to get kind of deep up in here. They want to fuck with you, cause they feeling your vibe".

Dre twisted up his face and said, "Yeah, but I don't want to fuck with them niggas like that".

"Dre you don't have to hang with them niggas 24/7 like you did with me. All I'm saying is just give them a big portion of the phone time so they'll be comfortable. And when you leave you just pass the torch off to them and they can take it from there".

Dre smirked and said, "I guess you right. Black if this is your first time in jail, then how the hell do you know so much about this shit?"

Black Cee chuckled and said, "Come on son, I'm from Brownsville. Never ran, never will. Half my projects got jail stories. I just paid attention when niggas were talking".

"On The Count!" A female c.o. announced from the front of the dorm causing everyone to pause and waited from her to do a head count. When she got to the back of the dorm where Dre and Black Cee were sitting, she looked at Cee and said, "Smith you ready?"

"If you the one that's walking me out the front door, then I'm ready when you are", Black Cee said with a sly smirk on his face.

She rolled her eyes and said, "Just be ready in five minutes".

When she walked away Black Cee said, "Yeah, she's on my dick".

Dre burst out laughing, "Yo Cee you the illest…I'm going to miss you dawg".

"Smith let's go!"

Dre gave his friend a pound and a hug for a final time. "You know where to find me. If you need anything just get at me", Black Cee said before walking off and out of the dorm.

Chapter 31

With Dre locked up and Fat Pee always tied up with this chick or that situation, De'Quan knew it was up to him to find their next vic. Problem was vics just don't fall out of the sky. He came across a couple of prospects, but nothing solid. To get his mind off of his mounting problems, De'Quan decided to take as solo trip to club Esso's. Cursing through New York City clubs on a late night always gave De'Quan a rush and when the streets are bubbling, if you listen close enough, you may be able to pick up some valuable information.

Club Esso's was a two story structure that gave you a comfortable sense of being in a hip-hop lounge, with a full bar, and section off booths for a more interment setting. The dance floor downstairs jammed to the new 112 feat. Biggie song as De'Quan moved through the crowd and headed upstairs to look in on the mini stage performance they had going for the night.

Mic Geronimo and Royal Flush had the second floor bouncing to their street anthem as De'Quan made his way to the crowded bar to order a double Hennessey.

"Oh I'm sorry".

De'Quan turns around to see who just bumped into him and he was taken aback by the beauty he just came face to face with. De'Quan smiled, "That's okay, yo trying to order something?"

The girl looked at him up and down and quickly sized De'Quan up. She returned the smile and said, "Yes, will yo help me out?" She waved her hands in a look at this motion.

De'Quan chuckled and said, "Yeah I know, I been trying to get a bar tender for a minute. I got you though, what you drinking?"

"Can you order me a red devil please?" She asked, batting her eyes and handing him a folded up bill.

"Nah, keep your money, this drink is on me", De'Quan said and turned around to get the bar tenders attention.

When De'Quan turned from the bar with the drinks the girl said, "thank you, but you didn't have to do this".

De'Quan smiled, "Don't worry about it; I'm sure you'll hit me back on the next round".

"You confident there's going to be a next round huh".

"Sure am…now what's your name sweetheart?"

"Melissa", she stuck out her hand to shake his. De'Quan took her hand and smoothly caressed hers, "and yours?"

"De'Quan. Who are you here with?"

"My girl friend and her boy-friend. They're downstairs, hugged up in a booth, so I came to check out the show up here. Who did you come with?" Melissa said as she sipped on her drink.

"I'm here by myself. I was out driving and this spot looked like it was popping from the outside", De'Quan said, than he looked around. "Do you want to sit down?"

"Sure". Melissa said. De'Quan took her hand into his and he led the way through the crowd to a small table with two empty chairs.

De'Quan and Melissa got lost in each other's conversation for over an hour, until it was suddenly broken up.

"There you are. I've been looking all over for you".

Melissa looked up and was surprised to see her friend standing there. "Oh I'm sorry, I thought you had company", Melissa joked.

"Well it looks like I'm breaking up your company. Hi, my name is Suge", she said with a bright smile and a wave.

De'Quan returned the smile and said, "I'm De'Quan. I'm sorry; I didn't mean to steal your friend like that".

"That's okay, but we are ready to leave now", Suge said looking over to Melissa.

Melissa frowned and said, "But I'm not finished yet".

De'Quan saw opportunity knocking and he knew he had to answer the door before it walked away. "I can take you home if you like".

Melissa's frown slowly started to fade, "Would you…that would be nice".

"Are you sure?" Suge asked with a skeptical look on her face.

"Girl I'll be fine", Melissa said in a reassuring tone.

"Trust me, she's in good hands", De'Quan said.

Suge looked him up and down, "Okay, you better make sure my friend gets home in one piece, or else I'm coming to find you. Where you from again?" Suge said with a smile, but De'Quan could tell she was serious about her inquiry.

"Don't worry, I'm not hiding, I'm from building 506 in Marcy projects", De'Quan said.

Suge laughed and gave Melissa a hug, "Okay. Melissa call me when you get in".

"Why, you not going to answer", Melissa joked.

"Yes I will, now call me".

"Okay, okay Mame. Now go", Melissa said as she kissed Suge on her cheek.

When Suge bounced back through the crowd, De'Quan said, "Now I feel at a disadvantage".

"Why is that?"

"Cause she knows where I live at, but I don't know where she's from".

Melissa chuckled, "I don't think you're going to give her a reason to come looking for you".

De'Quan laughed and said, "I'm not. You hungry?"

"A little".

"Cool, we can grab something on the way".

***** * * * *

"Thank you De'Quan, I really had a good ", Melissa said as they sat in his car out front of her building. "Suge pressed me to come out tonight, so I wasn't expecting to meet anyone, but I'm glad I did".

"No problem. You was good company for me, so I should be the one saying thank you", De'Quan said as he stared into her light brown eyes.

Melissa reached over and gave him a soft wet kiss that De'Quan found himself lost in. Melissa pulled back and said, "call me", as she hopped out of his car and skipped up the front steps of her building.

De'Quan watched Melissa's butt bounce under the skirt she was wearing and shook his head. "I'll be a fool not to call you", he said to himself as he put the car in drive and pulled away from the curb feeling like his realness is what won her over.

Chapter 32

Dre came home to less fan fare than he did when he had to turn himself in. Tammy waited on the other side of the Rikers Island Bridge for Dre to hop off of a transport bus. Dre's prison frown quickly turned into a smile when he saw his pregnant girl friend waiting for him by the bus stop.

"Hey baby", Dre said as he kissed her than kissed her big belly.

"We missed you so much", Tammy said as a tear slid out the corner of her eye.

Dre wiped it with his hand and said, "It's over now. Let's go home".

They hopped into a cab and took the Brooklyn-Queens expressway back to Brooklyn. Dre stared out of the window as they rode across the bridge and thought about how different the city looked across the East river after 6 months. His mind had been working in overdrive ever since the visit he had with De'Quan. No stash money, with a baby on the way, wasn't sitting well with Dre. He needed to get up with De'Quan and Fat Pee ASAP.

The cab navigated through the light traffic to Marcy houses, giving Dre a quick adrenaline rush. Even though he had only been gone for six months, it still felt like things had changed since he was gone. That is until Dre and Tammy stepped onto the elevator and the strong aroma of piss hit him. That's when he knew he was home.

Dre's mother was in the kitchen when she heard keys jiggling in the door. She put the top back onto the pot and turned around to greet her son. "Thank god you made it out of there, come let me look at you".

Dre chuckled and said, "Let me find out you were looking for me Ma".

They hugged and she took a step back to look her son up and down, "I was. You hungry, I made you something".

Dre laughed and said, "You cooked, it must going to snow today".

"If I wasn't so happy to see you, I would pop you over your head", She said then pushed him to the side. "Hey Tammy, how's my grand-baby doing in there?"

Tammy smiled as they hugged and said, "Acting crazy in there. I think cause I'm hungry".

"Oh ok, well grand-ma is almost finish in here".

"Oh so you didn't come home to see me, huh", Shakia said as she came down the hall.

Dre's face lit up, "Stop playing sis, what's up", he said as he gave her a big hug.

"Damn I missed you", Dre said.

"I missed you too".

"Well enough of the mushy stuff, yah get cleaned up and ready to eat, I'm going to start fixing these plates before my Grand-baby starts having another fit up in there", they all laughed and headed to the bathroom to wash their hands.

Blunt smoke seeped out of the windows as De'Quan whipped his Lexus down the Conduit expressway, going from Brooklyn to Sunrise. It was Dre second day home and it was time to take him shopping. De'Quan talked over the music about his late night encounter with the Spanish beauty he met at club SOS, in-between pulls of the blunt, before passing it off to Fat Pee.

"Yo son, if I wasn't so Moet'd up, I would have cared about crashing my shit!" All three friends laughed on cue.

Fat Pee took a pull of the blunt, and said, "Yo she got any freaky ass sisters, or is she one of a kind?"

De'Quan switched lanes as they came up on Green Ackers mall, "I don't know son, she left me downstairs on some call me later shit. I wasn't mad though".

For most of the ride to Queens Dre sat in the backseat, taking pulls of the blunt, lost in his own thoughts. Coming home to pressure of having a baby, with no real plan on how he was going to make some money was starting to get to Dre. Tammy was a solid trooper and was very understanding, but Dre knew he had to set her and the baby up proper.

"So how we gonna do this?" Dre asked, breaking up the laughter coming from the front seats of the car.

"We looking at some new spots now", Fat Pee said, as De'Quan navigated through the parking lot in search of a spot. "I'm trying to get up with this Spanish chick from Bushwick; she knows some info on this cat getting it on the dope tip".

"Oh yeah, what's his name?" De'Quan asked.

"Some cat named Diablo", Fat Pee said.

De'Quan found a spot, put the car in park, and lit up a cigarette. "I've been looking around uptown. We hit something up there, it's going to be worth it, you dig. That's why I've been taking my time. I have a feeling about that chick Melissa I met the other night. Cause shorty lives right on 140th street, you know any chick living on a block getting money like that one 9 times out of 10 she's holding something for somebody".

"Word", Fat Pee agreed, "Them dudes are getting money on that block".

Dre shook his head in agreement, "I heard about that block in jail".

"Well whatever route we go, we got to do this soon, cause I'm not trying to have my nephew coming out here hungry", Fat Pee said.

Dre smiled and De'Quan said, "Don't worry; something is going to pop off. Now let's go get my boy fresh".

"That's what I'm talking about", Dre said, cheeseing as they hopped out of the car and bounced to the mall.

Inside Dre made it his business to find some fresh feet's in Footlocker, while Fat Pee played the outside of the store trying to get a caramel complexion cutie number. De'Quan sat down, and then checked his beeper. A number came up he didn't recognize.

"Yo Dre, I'll be back, I'm going to the payphone", De'Quan said, as he passed Dre three hundred dollars and walked out of the store.

"Hello?"

"Yeah, somebody beeped me from this number?" De'Quan said.

"Is this De'Quan?" The soft sultry voice on the other end of the line asked.

"It all depends on who this may be", De'Quan playfully spat.

"Ahh, good one playboy, this is Melissa", She said as she lounged on her couch, dressed in a wife-beater and shorts. "I was hoping you didn't forget the sound of my voice so fast".

De'Quan chuckled, "Nah, I knew it was you".

"Okay, so are you busy?" Melissa asked.

"At the moment I'm out with my boy, but if you're not busy when I'm done I can come pick you up and treat you to a steak or something", De'Quan said, feeling confident Melissa won't turn down a steak dinner.

Melissa smiled and said, "That all depends on what time is later".

"Not too late, but late enough to make it a dinner date if you like".

"I like the sound of that", Melissa said smiling from ear to ear.

Chapter 33

De'Quan parked by the fire hydrant close to the front of Melissa's building and watched the activity that flowed from stoop to stoop on her block. Look outs on every corner braved the cold night air as people coming through to re-up either walked up or pulled into the block to purchase their product. De'Quan kept one hand on his 40caliber resting on the side of his seat, as his eyes bounced from mirror to mirror watching the action around him.

It was no secret Melissa lived on one of the most popular blocks in Washington heights when it came to who had the best product in New York City. The problem De'Quan thought to himself is robbing something on the block, then trying to get off of it. Fat Pee was a good driver, but De'Quan knew if any of the look outs got word something was going wrong inside of the building, they would have a major problem trying to get out of there.

After ten minutes of waiting Melissa came strutting out of the building in a pair of knee high boots. Her jeans defined every curve she possessed in the back, and she made sure it all showed under the waist high fur jacket she wore. When she got into the car De'Quan smiled and said, "You look nice".

"Thank you Poppy", She said as she reached over and gave him a soft kiss.

"That tasted good, you hungry?" De'Quan asked he pulled away from the curb.

"Starving, where we going?" Melissa asked as she leaned forward and De'Quan caught it out the side of his eye.

"Don't touch nothing".

Melissa burst out laughing and said, "How did you know I was going to touch something?"

"I felt the vibe that my radio space was about to be invaded".

"Okay I won't touch, unless you want me too", Melissa said.

De'Quan smiled and said, "I want you to touch, but not the radio". They laughed and joked all the way downtown. De'Quan took Melissa to Tad's steak house in the heart of Times Square.

When they finished their meals, they sat at the table staring at each other over drinks until Melissa said, "So tell me something good about yourself".

"Wow that's' a good question. Well off the top of my head, I would have to say I treat people the way they want to be treated. A person shows me love, then I'm going to return that love. What about you, what do you do all day, like do you have a job that takes up most of your days and nights?"

Melissa took a sip of her drink and said, "I work as a receptionist for a firm who represents clients like American Express, and AT&T. Real boring stuff. What about you Mr. Lexus".

De'Quan chuckled and said, "Right now I'm not doing anything until I start this tech school, and having a Lexus in New York is nothing. Now if I was pushing a helicopter, then that would be a major thing. So who do you live with?"

She shifted in her seat and said, "I'm on my own, why, you curious about what goes on upstairs?"

Her voice was more intoxicating to De'Quan, than the glass of Hennessey he was sipping on. "Only if you want me too".

Melissa smiled, "I might".

De'Quan felt it. That was his cue to get the bill and get her into the warm car as soon as possible. When they were in the car De'Quan asked, "You ever smoked Hydro?"

"Not yet, why you have some?" Melissa asked.

De'Quan smiled as he pulled the car out onto the flow of traffic, "No, but the one of the few spots in the city is a few blocks from your house".

Melissa knew what he had in mind, but she didn't protest. She just leaned back and enjoyed the smooth ride back uptown.

De'Quan stopped at the weed spot on 145th street, dipped into the store next door to grab them some junk food and juices, and then drove over to 140th street. Even though it was close to 12 o'clock at night, the action on Melissa's block was still going. As he parked the car a thought hit De'Quan, maybe they can follow somebody after they pick up their work from Melissa's block. If they did it like that, they avoid getting into drama with the guys hustling on her actual block. He put the thought in the back of his mind and they headed upstairs.

When they were safely in Melissa's apartment, she instructed De'Quan to have a seat on a beige leather sofa, while she hung up their coats and put on the radio. De'Quan quickly took in his surroundings, as he got comfortable. Melissa lived in a one bedroom apartment on the third floor of a five story walk-up. Being that Melissa lived in a high crime area De'Quan figured her rent couldn't be that much. The inside of her apartment told a different story.

Across from the leather sofa he was sitting on was a matching loveseat, and a glass coffee table in-between. A 40in TV rested in the middle of a wooden wall unit. Pictures of Melissa and her family hung on the walls and De'Quan immediately got the feeling she didn't just let people into her home unless she was comfortable. He pulled out the weed and handed it to her when she came back into the living room.

188

"So this is the famous Hydro. I've heard about it, but I've haven't had it yet. Is it true they grow this weed under water?" Melissa asked as she sat down on the couch next to him.

"Yeah, in fish tanks and shit", De'Quan said as he pulled out a Dutch master and started breaking it open.

"I hope this Hydro is all that like you and everybody is saying it is, or else we gonna have a problem up in here".

De'Quan laughed as he watched her get up and put on her slippers, then put on the sexy sounds of SWV on the stereo. "If this shit don't hit you like the Hulk, then I'll break out and leave you untouched. How about that".

She laughed as she lit up an incense and brought two glasses of water to the table. "Oh really, you must be really confident about that lah. I hope you're that confident in other areas".

"Oh believe me, I won't disappoint", De'Quan smoothly said, then pulled out his lighter and passed them to her.

"Oh I get to do the honors", Melissa said with a big smile.

"It's your castle, so it's only right", De'Quan said.

She got up and handed it back to him, "That's okay, you can spark it. I want to put on a movie. Have you ever seen 'Tales from the Hood' before?"

"Nah. I've heard of it though", De'Quan said as he lit up the blunt and watched her open up a lower compartment on the wall unit and pull out a couple of video tapes. Melissa shuffled threw the collection in her hands. From the angle he was sitting on the couch, De'Quan's eyes began to stare at a grey package resting in the back of the compartment. The smoke went down his throat hard and De'Quan went into a coughing fit.

She turned around with a big smile and said, "You need some help?"

"Oh yeah", De'Quan said laughing in-between his coughing.

Melissa put the movie on and closed up the compartment. When she sat back down, he passed her the blunt and after four deep pulls, the lah caught her in her throat. Melissa's coughing fit was worst than De'Quan's. Her eyes began to water and De'Quan thought he saw snot coming out of her nose. Melissa put the blunt in the ash tray and dipped off to the bathroom.

De'Quan began to laugh, "I guess I'll smoke this by myself".

De'Quan lit up the blunt, then a thought hit him. He looked over his shoulder than quickly moved to the wall unit. He opens up the compartment and pulled out what he thought was a package, and he was right. De'Quan put the package back, then calmly sat back down on the couch with a hundred things started racing through his mind as he waited for Melissa to come out of the bathroom.

Melissa came back into the livingroom with an embarrassing grin on her face. She sat down on the couch and reached for the blunt.

"Oh you think you ready for round two champ", De'Quan said with a slight chuckle.

"Shut up", Melissa joked as she took the blunt and they relaxed into a smooth smoking rhythm while they watched the movie. As the movie progressed, they moved in close to each other, which lead to some light four play.

"Hold on a sec", Melissa said as she hopped up off of the couch and stepped in the back again.

De'Quan thought about the package Melissa had in the bottom of her wall unit, and he had to stop himself just taking it and leaving her house before she came from out the back. That would make him look petty and De'Quan knew if Melissa had one, then she had access to a lot more. If it wasn't in her house already.

Melissa walked back into the livingroom dressed in a Victoria Secret oriental style, thigh high, silk robe, with her hair draped down to her shoulders. De'Quan took one look at Melissa and his manhood almost burst out of his pants. The look in Melissa's eyes was one of pure experience as she got down on her knees in front of him and in a low seductive voice she said, "How do you want it?"

De'Quan smiled and said, "However you want to give it, your house, your moves".

Melissa smiled and began to undo his pants, smoothly releasing De'Quan's aching hard-on. De'Quan grabbed the remote control and put the TV on mute. Then he pressed play on the CD player button. Total blared out of the speakers asking the world can't we see, what he's doing to them, as De'Quan began to relax and let Melissa suck on him like she found her long lost lollypop. De'Quan had to smile to himself because he knew he hit the jackpot with Melissa.

Chapter 34

"Man I can't wait till we on that college campus, all the girls are going to be checking for the Brooklyn kid, with the nice handle", Jamel said as he bounced the basketball between his legs, then drove to the basket for an uncontested lay-up.

Ne'Sean picked up the rebound and said, "Who me? Cause I'm the only Brooklyn kid I know with a nice handle".

Ne'Sean took a 12 foot jump shot that went in. Jamel passed the ball back to Ne'Sean, then grabbed the rebound when Ne'Sean missed on his second attempt. Out the corner of his eye, Ne'Sean saw his girlfriend Karmen coming into the park with her two friends Adina and Mimi.

Karmen was looking comfortable in a beige velour suit with a pair of 5411 Reebox on her feet. Her black Pelle Pelle jacket was open halfway giving Ne'Sean the invitation to put his hands inside and hug and kiss Karmen all in one motion.

"What's up baby, I'm sorry, I lost track of the time", Ne'Sean said with his winning smile.

Karmen rolled her eyes, "Oh yeah, I see I had to come down here and get your ass. I told you I had to talk to you", Karmen said with a slight frown on her face.

Adina smacked the ball out of Jamel hands and said, "How you suppose to win in college when you can't even hold onto the ball in an empty park?"

Mimi snickered as Jamel tried to take the ball back from Adina, "Don't worry about that, I'll bust your ass". Being a tomboy Adina loved to intimidate other kids in the projects, especially the boys.

"Yeah right Jamel, you too little homeboy", Adina said as she began to back Jamel down to the basket and lay up the ball for two. Mimi hollered in laughter as Jamel ran after the rebound and slipped on some dirt.

Ne'Sean and Karmen walked away from the ruckus on the court to sit down on the benches. Ne'Sean hopped onto the bench back support, as Karmen leaned in between his legs. The young couple had been seeing each other for the past seven months, and they never had a beef with each other because Ne'Sean had a dream and Karmen was all for it.

Ne'Sean knew Karmen well enough to know when something was wrong with her, he lightly pushed her back to look into her eyes and asked, "What's wrong Karmen?"

She didn't know how to tell him what has been on her mind, "Sean my period has been late for a month now", she said hoping he would catch the hint from that piece of information.

He didn't.

"What does that mean, you hurt or something?"

She shifted her weight and said, "I did one of those home tests and…" Karmen let her words trail off as she watched his reaction.

It slowly started to hit Ne'Sean and his facial expressing began to change, "But I used a condom…Ahh man, Naw. What you saying Karmen, cause we used a condom".

A mist began to form up in her eyes as she said, "I know Sean, that's the same thing I said in the bathroom this morning, but then I remembered the few times the condom broke and I started to cry. I'm sorry Sean".

A million things began to flow through his mind all at once. Ne'Sean didn't know how he should take this news. In those short moments, it took everything in him not to flip on Karmen and blame this whole mess on her. She knew he was about to go to U.N.C. in the summer and something like her being pregnant can derail his whole plan to get his family out of the hood with his talent. They spoke about this.

"Ne'Sean say something", Karmen whined, snapping Ne'Sean out of his trance.

"Who else did you tell?" Ne'Sean asked looking over her shoulder at Adina and Mimi.

"Nobody Ne'Sean. Damn that's all you can say?"

"Karmen calm down, I'm trying to process this shit just like you".

"Damn why you got to curse at me?" Karmen asked looking genuinely hurt.

"Don't tell anybody about this, okay", Ne'Sean said ignoring her. "I'll get the money so you can go to one of those clinics".

"For what!" Karmen snapped as she pulled back from him. "I'm not getting an abortion Ne'Sean. You know that's against my religion. My mother will kill me".

"Okay, don't worry about it K, let me think about this and see what we can do without you violating your religion, and me losing my basketball scholarship. Let's just keep this to ourselves for now", Ne'Sean said as he looked into her light eyes.

A tear trickled out of her eyes and she quickly whipped at them. She nodded, "Okay".

Ne 'Sean kissed her and stood up, "Come on, I'll walk you home".

$$*****$$

Ne'Sean paced his room trying to think about what he was going to do with Karmen. They will never let him go away to college knowing he has a baby on the way. He needed a plan or else everything he worked hard for will end at the drop of a dime.

He paced his room thinking about all the possible scenarios that could go down once they announce Karmen is pregnant. It hit him this is a moment in time where he needed to talk to Pop, because he never judged them and always was willing to find a solution to one of his kid's problems. Not having Pop around for his prime young years was really hurting Ne'Sean on the inside. That's why he made basketball his focus for the last few years, and now he was facing the possibility of losing out on his opportunity to play on a larger stage than his New York City high school, and getting his family out of Marcy projects.

When he was tired of pacing his room Ne'Sean sat down on the bed and started counting off all the people in his life who is going to scream at him for getting Karmen pregnant. He couldn't think of anyone who will give them their blessings to have a baby. This was something he needed to take care of on his own. Ne'Sean reached down under the bed and pulled out a Timberland box. He open it and took out a small knot of money and a 32 caliber handgun.

194

This will just have to be a secret they take to the grave with them, because he couldn't risk it Ne'Sean said to himself as he counted out his last $487 dollars. Karmen will have to understand this one time they are going to have to do something nobody in the world but them and the doctor will know about.

Ne'Sean sneaked out of his apartment determine to make Karmen see things his way.

Chapter 35

De'Quan weaved through traffic, headed uptown on the Westside highway with the hard sounds of 'Only Built for Cuban Linx' knocking out of the Lexus Bose system. Ever since he saw the package of drugs in Melissa's house, De'Quan had been scheming on how he was going to get to the main stash.

Melissa was making it hard for him, and she didn't even know it. Whenever they were together, she would turn down answering her phone, making her movement centered around him and what they are doing. De'Quan could feel it though, that moment when Melissa is going to need him to take her somewhere other than the store.

When De'Quan pulled up in front of Melissa's building the usual activity with the neighborhood hustlers directing traffic into the building of choice to do their business. He parked and surprised to see Melissa coming out of the building carrying a black bag along with the Gucci bag she had draped over her shoulder. De'Quan's heart skipped a beat as she got into the car and gave him a quick kiss on his lips.

"Hi popi, can you do me a favor and take me to my cousin house on 160 street and Broadway?" Melissa asked with a smile no man could resist.

"Oh okay, you want to stay over there or something?" De'Quan asked as he pulled the car from the curb.

"No. He wants me to bring him something. So I was thinking we could grab something from the fish market, maybe", Melissa said.

De'Quan had to maintain his composer. He just was thinking about a shot at seeing where the real work was at, and now that it looked like he was about to get some answers, De'Quan was feeling real jumpy on his insides.

"Ok that sounds cool, you looking tasty in those jeans", De'Quan said as he looked from the road to her thighs.

Melissa blushed and said, "Keep your eyes on the road Mister".

"Si Mame".

De'Quan drove up to 160th street and found a parking spot in-between Amsterdam and Broadway. Melissa readied herself to get out of the car and De'Quan knew he had to think fast.

"I have to use the bathroom".

Melissa froze as if she was thinking about what to do next. "I will only be a second. You can't hold it?"

"I been holding it ever since I left Brooklyn", De'Quan said with some discomfort on his face.

"Okay, come on", she said getting out of the car.

They stepped into the five story walk-up with De'Quan looking at everything there was to memorize about the building and anyone hanging out in front. The first two doors sported broken locks, which wasn't uncommon in the high crime area. They climbed the stairs to the third floor which had four apartments on the landing. Melissa knocked on apartment 3C and waited. De'Quan felt some movement behind the door and an eye appeared I the peephole. Seconds later the door swung open and a big brown skin man with a thick beard stood in the doorway sizing De'Quan up.

He asked Melissa something in Spanish and she replied with a smile which seemed to soften the man up.

"Okay, the bathroom is over here", the man said in a heavy accent.

De'Quan nodded his head as he walked into the apartment and headed for the bathroom. Melissa went into the back of the apartment while the big man at the door closed it and waited in the short hallway.

Once De'Quan closed the bathroom door, he went to the window and looked out of it to see where the apartment was located from a window view. The window was in the back of the building, and from where he was standing, there was no way for anybody to get in through the windows. He turned to the toilet and peed, then stood still for a moment to catch the voices he was hearing coming from the other side of the wall.

The lingo was in Spanish, causing De'Quan to curse himself under his breath for never sticking around in his Spanish classes in high school. He flushed the toilet, and then stepped back out into the hallway where the big doorman was patiently waiting. De'Quan half nodded his head and said "Thanks man". He pointed toward the bathroom.

The man just stared at De'Quan and let out a deep grunt. De'Quan looked down the hallway but all he could see was half open doors. Seconds later Melissa came out of one of the back rooms and smiled when she saw De'Quan was ready.

"Thank you Bolo", Melissa said to the doorman, then gave him a light kiss on his cheek.

Bolo grunted again and kept his eyes on De'Quan the whole time as he let them out.

When they were back in the car De'Quan said, "I see he's light on conversation".

Melissa chuckled and said, "He only talks when money is involved ".

De'Quan pulled his car out into ongoing traffic, then took a shot in the dark and asked, "What if I wanted to cop some grams from them?"

Melissa was quiet for a moment as she studied the side of his face. "I didn't know you messed with coke".

"Only if my money get's low. My Pops went to jail for selling it, so that's why I don't use it as an everyday job", De'Quan said as he kept his eyes on the road.

Melissa looked like she was in deep thought, so De'Quan let her be as he weaved through the streets and headed to an Italian restaurant on 88th street.

"I'll ask Bolo, but you have to be getting something big, or he won't want to do it", Melissa said once De'Quan parked the car outside of the restaurant.

"I mean I don't have 2 brick money if that what you mean", De'Quan said with a big smile on his face.

Melissa chuckled and said, "I know you not going to want no two bricks silly. I'm saying anything less than a quarter key they not going to want to mess with". She sat back to watch his reaction. Melissa wasn't sure about how much money De'Quan was handling, but him being interested in buying some work from her connection made her open up her ears a little wider.

"Ok, how much they charge for a half of key?" De'Quan asked as he finished parking then turned the car off.

Melissa didn't want to give off too much information like she knew the whole operation, "I'm not sure, they charge different. Sometimes it's ten thousand, sometimes nine. I will ask them later. Can we go eat something now?" She joked as they climbed out of the car.

"Anything for that sexy ass accent", De'Quan said as he caught a wind of something real was about to happen in the next few days.

Chapter 36

With so much going on in his life Ne'Sean was beginning to feel like the universe was going against him. Ne'Sean grew up believing every since Pop went to prison it would be on him to get his family out of the projects. Ne'Sean's world revolved around playing basketball. Taking his game to the next level had been his goal once they knew Pop wasn't coming home for a long time.

He knew running with his brother and his friend's wasn't the answer they were looking for to making it out of the projects, and lately Ne'Sean had been keeping his distance from them. Dividing up his time between practicing on the court, helping out Mama K at the store, or hanging out with Karmen. Now that was beginning to look like a bad move, because now Karmen was pregnant. Having a baby was nowhere in his plans, and he had to rectify the situation with her before the wrong person found out about their secret.

Karmen hadn't heard from Ne'Sean in two days and she was beginning to worry he wouldn't want to talk to him anymore because she told him she was pregnant and didn't believe in abortions.

Karmen waited to ten o'clock and when she hadn't heard from him all day again, she decided to go looking for him.

"I'll be back in a little while Ma", Karmen said called out down the hallway as she put on her coat.

"Okay, don't stay out too late", her mother answered as she turned her attention back to her TV show.

Karmen stepped out into the hallway, locked the door, and then was suddenly startled when she saw Ne'Sean standing in the shadows of the building staircase.

"Oh shit Sean, you scared me. What are you doing standing there?"

When Ne'Sean stepped out of the shadows he was wearing a blue hoody, and Karmen noticed he had beads of sweat forming on his forehead even though it was cold in the hallway.

"Come on let's go up to the roof and talk", Ne'Sean said as he led the way up the stairs. Karmen hesitated before following him up the two flights to the roof. When they reached the top, Ne'Sean walked over to the edge and looked down to the front of the building. Karmen walked out onto the roof and immediately felt the cold night breeze brush across her smooth face.

"Sean what's going on?" Karmen asked as she pulled her coat together and hugged herself.

Ne'Sean turned around and said, "We're not having a baby".

His straight face with no chaser scared Karmen, but backing down to this life changing decision, that she wasn't going to do. "What are you talking about? You can't just make that decision without talking to me Ne'Sean".

"Look, I can't have a baby right now. I'll lose my scholarship, and I can't do that", Ne'Sean said wiping the sweat from his forehead with his bare hand.

Karmen snapped, "Scholarship? Nigga fuck a scholarship. So what am I suppose to do Sean, you know it's against my religion to have an abortion".

Ne'Sean shook his head in denial as he stepped closer to her and said, "Karmen, we're not having the baby".

Karmen was in a rage, "You know what Ne'Sean, fuck you. I'm having this baby, and if your punk ass don't want to help me then you'll pay for that shit".

She turned on her heels and headed toward the roof door. Ne'Sean's reflex's kicked into gear and he grabbed Karmen by her arm with one hand, and pulled out the gun with his free hand.

Karmen saw the gun, but it didn't register that Ne'Sean was threaten to use it to harm her. "Get the fuck off of me Sean".

"You can't have this baby Karmen", Ne'Sean said as they began to tussle. Karmen tried to pull away causing her to slip on the gravel laced roof. Ne'Sean lost his balance and fell forward into Karmen.

Boom

When the shot went off Ne'Sean's heart skipped a beat as Karmen eyes looked to be frozen in time. They crumbed to the ground and Ne'Sean quickly scrambled to his feet. "Oh no, no, no. Karmen get up baby", Ne'Sean pleaded as tears began to form in his eyes.

Karmen's body went limp, and a voice in Ne'Sean's head told him to run. He tried to pick her up, but Karmen wasn't moving. Ne'Sean quickly looked around then bust through the roof door, taken the stairs two at a time as he headed for the lobby.

"Yo motherfucker, watch where you going", A neighborhood dealer barked as he made a sale to a crack head.

"Sorry", Ne'Sean mumbled as he sprinted out of the building and headed straight home.

✳✳✳✳✳
___

Ne'Sean sat under the dim light of his bedroom rocking back and forth, with tears streaming down his cheeks. He could not believe he just shot his high school sweetheart. Ne'Sean told himself over and over again, 'It was an accident'; he never meant to hurt Karmen. Ne'Sean knew no one will ever believe him, making the tears come down even harder. He needed to get himself together and come up with a plan.

201

Looking down on the floor Ne'Sean stared at the 32 revolver resting in between his feet. 'I need to get rid of this gun', he told himself. Before he could come up with a solid course of action, he heard a knock at the door and almost jumped out of his boots.

Mama K and Meika were asleep, and Ne'Sean hadn't seen De'Quan in days. He grabbed the gun off of the floor and crept to the front door. Ne'Sean's heart was beating a mile a minute as one hundred bad thoughts ran through his mind. One thing was for sure, if that is the police knocking at the door, he wasn't trying to go to jail. The thought of going out like this made Ne'Sean grip the handle of the gun a little tighter, as he put his ear to the door and listened for any sounds of voice's and walkie-talkie's. He didn't hear any.

He slowly slid the peep-hole to the side and was surprised to see Dre standing in the hallway. Ne'Sean tried to calm his nerves as he put the gun in his pocket and slowed his breathing down before opening up the door.

"You alright man?" Dre asked looking at the beads of sweat rolling down the side of Ne'Sean's face.

"What? Yeah. What you want, De'Quan ain't here", Ne'Sean said wiping his forehead with his bare hand.

"I know", Dre said as he looked around the hallway. When Ne'Sean didn't invite him in Dre gave him the rest of the story. "He called me. He said to come and get you, he needs to see us".

Ne'Sean thought about it, than open the door wider to let Dre in. The hallway was dark as they made their way down to the bedroom. Dre sat on the bed as Ne'Sean closed the door and stood up. Dre was used to Ne'Sean acting weird sometimes, but as he analyzed Ne'Sean standing over by the door he realized he was fully dressed at 1:30 in the morning.

"You were going somewhere?" Dre asked.

Ne'Sean shifted in his stance and said, "Nah. What's up man? I haven't seen De'Quan in days. You said he called you, what did he say?"

Dre brushed off Ne'Sean's funny behavior and got down to business. "He said he was working on something uptown, and he needs us to come up there tonight".

Ne'Sean let Dre's word sink in as the thought's of the police knocking on the door any moment now crept into his mind. Snapping out of his trance Ne'Sean saw this as an opportunity to get out of the house and get up with his brother and tell him what happened between him and Karmen.

"Oh ok".

"Yo you sure you alright man? You don't look too good", Dre said staring at Ne'Sean as he stood in the shadows of the room.

Wiping the sweat from his forehead and wiping his hand on his sweatshirt, Ne'Sean quickly brushed him off. "Yeah man, you think we need some heat?"

"He might just want us to come and check it out, but to be on the safe side yeah let's bring some.

* * * * *

Marty Mar and Bliss took the stairs two at a time, instead of waiting for the slow elevator. When they reached the roofs landing Marty Mar sat down on the steps, while Bliss remained standing as he caught his breath.

Marty Mar and Bliss were on roll tonight. They just coped from the dealer in the lobby after robbing another person for their wallet. Two fat wallets in one night gave them the options to do big things with the rest of their night. Bliss pulled out the fresh wallet they took from a Chinese delivery man and began to fidget with its contents, as Marty Mar pulled out his stem and began to stuff it with a few crack rocks.

"How much is in that one?" Marty Mar asked as he looked from the stem to the wallet.

Bliss sucked his teeth and said, "Shit, this motherfucker only had 47dollars and some loose change in one of these small pockets. Man what's taking you so long to load that shit up?"

"Shhh, man fuck you being so loud for? When it's your turn to go first, I don't rush you. So B-E-Z greasy". Marty Mar said as he pulled out his lighter and put the flame to the end of the stem.

Bliss turned his attention back to the wallet, "Damn this nigga had some ugly ass kids".

Marty Mar chocked on the smoke as Bliss threw down the wallet and snatched the stem out of Marty Mar's hand. "Man give me that!"

Bliss put the light to the pipe and as he took a long pull of the crack smoke he got a strange feeling, he was hearing something.

"Yo did you hear that?" Bliss asked as he blew the smoke out. His eyes where bigger than an owl as he looked around the walls of the staircase.

Feeling like Bliss was trying to pull a fast one on him, Marty Mar reached to snatch the pipe out of his hand, "What is that, a joke? Nigga pass the pipe".

"No Shhh". Bliss said, and that's when Marty Mar heard it too.

"What the fuck was that?" Marty Mar asked as he stood up and looked down the stairwell. They both stood in silence as they waited for the sound again.

When they heard the sound again, Marty Mar turned to the roof door and pulled it open. Karmen was half conscious as she tried to raise her head. Bliss freaked out and dropped the stem.

"Oh shit man, I told you we shouldn't have used this staircase", Bliss blurted out as he stared at Karmen.

"Shut up stupid, you broke the got damn stem", Marty Mar snapped. He turned around and reached down to help Karmen up.

"Man don't touch that bitch. Your finger prints are going to be all over her", Bliss snapped as he nervously looked around.

"Man shut up, I saw her around here. She's from out here", Marty Mar said as he pulled Karmen from out of the cold and onto the roof landing. She was still alive, but barely.

Bliss couldn't careless as he picked up the broken pieces of the stem and the wallet and said, "Alright man, that's it. Now leave her right there, and we can call somebody downstairs.

Marty Mar shook his head, "Nah you go, and I'll stay with her".

"What? Are you crazy?"

"Man just go call an ambulance from the corner, and hurry up", Marty Mar snapped as he put Karmen's head in his lap.

"Alright…alright", Bliss said, turning on his heels and sprinting down the stairs.

✶✶✶✶✶

When Dre open the car door waking Fat Pee up out of a heavy nod, he wiped the drool from the corner of his mouth. "Damn man, what took yah so long?"

Dre hopped into the front seat, as Ne'Sean climbed into the back. "We didn't take that long. Let's go", Dre said.

Fat Pee stared up the car then looked into the rear view mirror, "What's up Ne'Sean?"

Ne'Sean turned his attention from looking out the window, "Nothing".

Fat Pee put the car in drive and pulled out of the spot; he drove around to the Flushing side of the projects and cruised pass some police activity that was taking place in front of Karmen's building. Ne'Sean slowly eased back in his seat as he saw the EMT's wheeling somebody into the back of the ambulance.

"Damn I wonder who that is", Dre said.

Fat Pee kept his attention on the road as Ne'Sean mumbled, "I don't know".

Dre shook it off and turned on the radio. They listen to the late night sounds of Hot97 as they road up to Washington Heights to meet up with De'Quan.

$$*****$$

De'Quan had always been a light sleeper, even after a heavy love scene he just put together with Melissa. He lay back staring at the ceiling and listened to the steady rhythm of Melissa's breathing. For the last hour Melissa sound like she was in a heavy sleep. De'Quan smoothly eased his way out of the bed and grabbed his clothes off of the floor. He crept out of the bedroom and went into the livingroom to get dressed. Sitting down on the couch De'Quan stared at Melissa's wall unit as he put on his pants.

The last time De'Quan took a sneak peek into Melissa's wall unit he came face to face with a package that looked to be a little over a half of key. He put the rest of his stuff on, stood in silence for a few moments before opening up the bottom compartment of the wall unit.

De'Quan pulled out a small paper bag and quickly opened it. He counted out five wrapped up packages that couldn't have been more than an ounce of cocaine each.

De'Quan sucked his teeth and put the small package back. That small amount of drugs wasn't going to solve their money problems.

De'Quan let himself out of the apartment and headed outside to his car.

✶✶✶✶✶

"Hey Billy wake up. Check this out", Todd said to his sleeping partner.

Billy wakes up and quickly try's to focus on what Todd was pointing at. "I wonder where he's going".

"I don't know. You think we should follow him?"

"Yeah, let's see where lover boy is going in the middle of the night", Billy said as he started up the car and began to follow De'Quan.

✶✶✶✶✶

De'Quan drove to 154th street and parked in the 24 hour parking garage, then walked two blocks over to meet up with his brother and two friends, "What's happening?" De'Quan said when he hopped in the back of jeep. He gave everybody a pound and sat back in his seat.

"You tell us. Must be something good you got us out here in the middle night", Dre said feeling restless.

"Word Quan what gives, you found something?" Fat Pee asked.

De'Quan looked around the car and said, "Yeah, remember shorty I've been fucking with from uptown?"

Everybody in the car slightly nodded. De'Quan continued, "Well she took me to her connect about two weeks ago, and I brought some shit from them. I got rid of the work and came back to them".

"Word, so when were you going to tell us that?" Dre asked with some distaste in his voice.

"When I knew for sure we could get up in the house without shorty's help", De'Quan shot back.

"Sounds like you really digging this chick", Dre said.

"Yo Dre I know you tight cause Rah lost our bread while you was gone", De'Quan said going at the root of Dre's attitude.

"You damn right I'm tight, and now Tammy is about to have this baby any day now and I don't even have any money to buy pampers", Dre said.

De'Quan broke the silence in the car, "Nigga, we brothers, so if you think we trying to have you have a baby with no bread to hold yah down then you're crazy. I ain't been around cause I've been working on this, and now I can get these niggas to open up the door without her".

"How much is in there?" Fat Pee asked to change the tone.

"At least two keys and some money", De'Quan said as everyone let his words soak in.

"How many dudes are up there?" Dre asked.

"Just two, one who answers the door and the other conducts the business in the livingroom", De'Quan reported.

"So you want to do this now?" Fat Pee asked.

"Shit why not. What's up Ne'Sean, you haven't said nothing yet", De'Quan said looking over to his brother.

Ne'Sean shifted in his seat and said, "Uh yeah, I'm good, whatever you want to do bro".

"If you not with this, Pee can come up stairs and up can stay in the car", De'Quan said, staring at his brother still not convinced he was ready.

"I'm good bro, and besides I can't drive like Pee can", Ne'Sean said.

"Okay, yah brought the guns right?" De'Quan said turning attention back to the task at hand.

"Yeah we got them", Dre said picking up the book-bag he had resting in between his feet and passing it to De'Quan.

De'Quan looked in the bag and said, "Okay cool. Let's do this, Pee drive to 160th street, in between Amsterdam and Broadway".

Fat Pee started up the jeep as De'Quan passed out the guns and everybody put on their game faces.

*****

The black car followed De'Quan to the parking garage, waited for him to come out, then followed him to a parked jeep and watched him get into the back seat.

"Wonder what he's doing", Todd said as the stared at the parked jeep. The two partners sat in silence for fifteen minutes, until the jeep suddenly started up and pulled out of its parking spot.

"Okay, let's go", Billy said putting the car in drive and following the black jeep down Broadway. When the jeep turned onto 160th street, Todd looked over to his partner with a worried look in his eyes.

"You think he's going up to the apartment without Melissa?"

Billy looked over to Todd when the jeep pulled over and parked by the hydrant and said, "He might. I think we should call it in".

They stared at the jeep for five minutes until they saw the passenger doors swing open with De'Quan and two other

men exit the car, and head into the building. "Yeah we should",
Billy said.

Todd grabbed the walkie-talkie and made the call.

Chapter 37

The telephone ringing woke her up out of a heavy sleep,
"Hello".

"Ms. Sanchez, this is Lieutenant Hardy", the deep voice
said.

Melissa tried to clear the cob webs as she sat up in the
bed and quickly looked around her dark bedroom. From the
silhouette of the moon coming through the window Melissa
could see she was alone.

"Ah, yes what's going on?"

"Seems like the guy you've been dating in on his way up
to the Carlito apartment with a couple of friends. Did you know
anything about this?" Lt. Hardy asked.

"No sir", Melissa quickly answered as she hurried out of
bed and threw on anything that was in arms distance.

"Okay, well we have a team out front of the building".

"Are they going to take them?" Melissa asked as she
pulled on a pair of sneakers.

"Well they will be followed and pulled over. If their clean then we will let them go", Lt. Hardy said.

"Okay, I'm on my way there", Melissa said as she hung up the phone and ran out the door looking like a hot mess.

$$* * * * *$$

As a light drizzle soaked the rotten apple, the stolen Jeep Cherokee rolled to a stop in front of building 57 on 160th street, between Broadway and Amsterdam Avenue. Everyone in the jeep had butterflies in their stomachs. That wasn't enough to stop tonight show.

"Check your watch Pee. We will be out of there in 5 minutes tops. When we go in, Sean you grab the money and drugs; Me and Dre will hold the spot down." De'Quan said looking down at his watch. It was 4:47a.m.

"Pee give us to 4:52."

Pee nodded, and then set his digital guess watch, as his three passengers hopped out of the jeep and headed for the front door of the five story walk-up. They took the steps two at a time all the way up to the fourth floor.

De'Quan held up his hand to motion to Dre and Ne'Sean, as they caught their breathes, then De'Quan eased up to the door and put his ear to it to listen for any sounds of movement on the other side. He heard a few voices that were rolling over the voices coming from the TV. De'Quan looked at Dre and Ne'Sean and nodded his head then pulled out his 40 caliber automatic. Dre and Ne'Sean followed suit by pulling out their own weapons and readied themselves for what was to come next.

De'Quan performed the secret knock he watched Melissa do earlier and took up his kick in the door stands, as Dre and Ne'Sean stood off to the side in anticipation. Suddenly an eye appeared in the peephole then quickly disappeared with the sound of the locks clicking from the other side.

Bolo snatched open the door surprised to see De'Quan there so late, "what do you..."

Bolo was cut off by the 40 caliber pistol which was shoved in his mouth with enough force to crack some of his front teeth. Dre wasted no time as he pushed past them and ran into the apartment with the fire raging bull and his eyes, "Get the fuck on the floor Poppy!"

A man sitting at a card table weighing some drugs flinched to grab the gun that was resting on the table, but Dre rushed in too fast and tackled the man out of his chair.

Ne'Sean was hot on Dre's heels when they ran into the backroom, and he paused with surprise when Dre tackled the man behind the table. Before Ne'Sean could react to the two tussling on the floor, the bedroom door suddenly swung open and the nose of a shotgun came charging out into the livingroom. Ne'Sean didn't think; he just pulled the trigger.

The man behind the shotgun took a shot in his arm and pulled his own trigger in the process sending out a loud bang that was deafening in the livingroom. Ne'Sean cried out in pain as he fell to the ground squeezing his trigger. When Ne'Sean hit the floor he dropped his gun and immediately grabbed for his leg.

The ruckus going on in the livingroom caused Bolo to try De'Quan. The second De'Quan took his eyes off of Bolo to look down the hallway; Bolo hit him with a left hook right in De'Quan's eye. The shock of being hit out of nowhere caused De'Quan to pull the trigger on his gun as he fell to the floor. Two bullets came out with one whizzing pass Bolo arm, but the second bullet ratcheted off of a pipe and hit Bolo in his neck. Bolo crumbled to floor grabbing at his neck.

De'Quan scrambled to his feet and watched as the life slowly poured out of Bolo's body. De'Quan stood still for a moment as he tried to focus. Bolo hit him so hard De'Quan was seeing two hallways. He tried to shake it off as he ran down the hallway and into the livingroom. Dre was off on one side pistol whipping a guy, while Ne'Sean laid in the middle of the floor gripping his leg. De'Quan quickly looked at the guy laying dead with his shotgun still in his hand, and then turned to his brother.

"Shit let me see", De'Quan said.

"Shit hurts man", Ne'Sean cried as sweat rolled down his forehead.

"I know man, don't worry, you going to be alright", De'Quan said.

Dre finished giving his victim a beat down that made the man pass out. He grabbed the bag off of the floor and started loading it up with anything he could get his hands on.

"Dre help me over here", De'Quan whined as he looked around the room for something to wrap around his brother wound.

Dre finished stuffing the bag with all the drugs and money he could take, and then he went into the back room to find a sheet, but he stopped and asked De'Quan, "What the hell happen to your eye?"

"Fucking dude sucker punched me, now can you go find something so we can get the fuck out of here", De'Quan snapped, visibly tight behind the growing shiner on his eye.

 Dre came out of the back room with a towel in one hand and a jacket in the other hand. He handed the towel to De'Quan and stood there staring at the jacket. De'Quan quickly wrapped the towel around Ne'Sean's leg then looked up at Dre.

"What's wrong man?" De'Quan asked as he and his brother looked up at Dre.

Dre turned the jacket around and on the back of it, it said N.Y.P.D.

"Where did you get that?" De'Quan asked with a scared look in his eyes.

"Out the back room man. Don't tell me these guys are five-o", Dre said.

De'Quan quickly snapped out of his trance and picked his brother up to his feet, "Come on, we got to get the fuck out of here".

*****

Melissa made the cab stop in the middle of the block and as she climbed out of it the first thing she saw that was out of order was the black jeep parked by the hydrant with its engine running.

Melissa stepped on to the curb and slowly put her hand into her purse. She slowly walked toward the building, but she keep her eyes on the jeep. Then suddenly the door to the building swung open and Dre came running out with De'Quan half carrying his brother as they hopped down the stairs.

Fat Pee watched Melissa get out of the cab and slowly walk up the hill towards the building, but he didn't think anything of it until Dre busted out the front of the building. Melissa stopped in her tracks and slowly pulled her gun out of her bag.

"Oh shit man, look out!" Fat Pee screamed as he raised the gun he had resting on the car floor and stuck it out the window.

De'Quan looked in Melissa's direction and froze in his tracks.

"Don't move De'Quan", Melissa said nervous about bumping into them on the sidewalk like this.

"Who's that man?" Ne'Sean asked with a nervous look in his eyes.

De'Quan looked from Melissa to Ne'Sean, then back to Melissa and said, "Nobody". Then De'Quan turned his gun in her direction and the quiet drizzlely night quickly turned into a shooting gallery.

Melissa dove out of the way and fell in between two parked cars. Dre threw the bag on the car floor as he jumped into the front seat and let off two shots into Melissa's direction.

"Come on man!" Dre barked, but his command was interrupted from the back end on the jeep as Todd and Billy let their presents be known in the gun fight. "Drop your weapons!"

De'Quan quickly pushed Ne'Sean into the backseat and Fat Pee couldn't wait any longer as he stepped on the gas with everyone screaming, "Come on man!"

De'Quan slipped when the jeep pulled off, causing him to hold onto the door for dear life as Fat Pee sped down the block heading for Broadway. Ne'Sean grabbed his brother and helped him get into the jeep, but their escape was cut short when Fat Pee drove the jeep onto Broadway and a police car heading to the scene clipped the back end of the jeep and sent it into a 360 spin into a parked car. The loud bang was deafening as the night sky was flooded by the sound of approaching sirens.

Dre was the first one in the jeep to react as he looked into the backseat. De'Quan and Ne'Sean were both knocked out by the impact. He looked at Fat Pee and said, "Shit man, we got to get out of here".

"I can't man, I'm stuck", Fat Pee said as he tried to pull his leg up from its stuck position in between the door and stirring wheel.

The police on the sidewalk slowly tried to make their way to the jeep but when they saw movement in the jeep everyone held their positions. Dre looked around and knew he had to make a move.

A tear slowly rolled down the side of Fat Pee's face as he read his friend mind and said, "Go head Dre, I'll hold you down".

Dre looked around the car one last time before nodding his head and snatching open the car door. Fat Pee stuck his gun out the shattered window and squeezed off as many shots as he could as Dre jumped out of the car and headed across Broadway. The gun fire was deafening in the early morning light as Dre weaved through two parked cars and hit the sidewalk on 162 street with full head of steam.

Dre could feel the heat on his back as he ran toward Riverside and hailed the first cab he saw cruising by. Dre snatched open the door and hopped into the backseat, "What's up Poppy, I'm going to Jersey".

The cab driver half turned to look over his shoulder and said, "New Jersey? No Poppy, that too far".

Dre quickly dug into the backpack and pulled out two hundred dollar bills, "Here Pop".

The cab driver looked at the money and slowly nodded, "Okay". He took the money from Dre then pulled away from the curb as the sirens got louder in the background. Dre kept his eyes in the rearview mirror as he watched two police cars come busting out of the block and headed south. The cab driver drove north and quickly connected to the highway toward the George Washington Bridge.

"Where you go?" The cab driver asked as he moved with flow of traffic.

Dre eased down in his seat and tried to calm his heart rate as he thought about his next move, "Take me to the Hilton by Newark airport".

"Muy bien".

When the cab driver dropped Dre off, he walked around the outside of the hotel and found another cab. He had the cab driver take him to a different hotel in Newark and he found a pay phone.

Tammy picked up on the forth ring, "Hello".

"Tammy I need you to get up right now", Dre said as he looked over his shoulder.

Tammy felt the seriousness in his voice and sat on her bed, "Dre what's wrong?"

"I need you to pack a bag and meet me in Jersey", Dre said.

"Huh, Jersey…baby what's going on?" Tammy said as she cut on her lamp and moved to the edge of her bed.

"I'll tell you when you get here, just hop in a cab and take it to the Ramada inn in south Newark", Dre said.

Tammy was quiet for a second before she sighed and said, "Okay".

"Tammy don't tell nobody where you going".

"Come on Dre its five o'clock in the morning, my mother is going to be looking for me before she goes to work. What am I suppose to say?" Tammy said feeling frustrated with Dre about this sudden call and move he wants her to do.

"Relax baby, just leave her a note, and say you'll call her later", Dre said.

Tammy thought about it, then got out of her bed, "Okay baby, I'm coming".

Chapter 38

De'Quan open up his eyes and the blurry vision he him feeling like he was on drugs. He tried to wipe his hand over his face, but was stopped in mid-motion by a strong set of handcuffs, that were connected to the hospital bed rail. His vision quickly began to clear as he looked around the room.

A uniform officer was sitting in the corner of the room writing in his note pad when he saw De'Quan wake up. He quickly got up and walked to the side of the bed, "Hey man how you feeling?"

"Like I got hit by a truck, where am I?"

"The hospital, what's your name?" The officer quickly asked.

"De'Quan."

"De'Quan what?" The officer asked in a concerned tone.

"Short. How did I get here?" De'Quan asked.

The officer looked toward the door, then back to De'Quan and said, "Hey hold on a second, somebody wants to talk to you".

The officer stuck his head out the door into the hallway and said, "He's up".

Before De'Quan could ask who was in the hallway the room was flooded by men in suits, a cameraman, and a nurse to quickly check his vital signs. The room buzzed with activity as the cameraman set up his camera, and a man in a blue suit took off his trench coat. He laid his coat on a chair and came over to the side of the bed.

"Hi, I'm ADA Mathew Stevens, and when he cuts on the camera I'm going to ask you a few questions about what happen last night on hundred and sixty First Street. First I will introduce myself, then you. Then I will ask you if you would like a lawyer present during this interview. If you do then we will turn the camera off and leave. If not then we will continue, okay", he said.

Before De'Quan could respond ADA Stevens turned to the cameraman and said, "Are we ready?"

"Yes sir", the camera man said as he put on his headphones and worked on the focus on the camera.

"Okay, quiet in the room please while we're taping", ADA Stevens said as he fixed his tie and put on his game face.

"Rolling", the cameraman said.

"I'm ADA Mathew Stevens from the District Attorney office of New York County. Today I am conducting an interview with", he looked down at a sheet of paper and quickly read the name off of it. "De'Quan Short. Mr. Short at this time I will ask you if you would like a lawyer present during this interview."

De'Quan looked around the room at all of the red and white faces and was immediately uncomfortable. Not one familiar face stared back at his. "Yes I need a lawyer".

ADA Stevens kept his cool as he said, "Cut the camera off".

The cameraman cut the camera off and everybody began to file out of the room under a mist of grumbles. ADA Stevens snatched his trench coat off of the chair and put his face close enough for De'Quan to see his nose hairs, "that's okay dick head, I tried to help you. I'll get the full story before the judge gives your ass 25years to life".

"Whatever fuck you too", De'Quan said.

ADA Stevens nodded his head and said; "Okay cool; let's go", and he and the rest of his entourage left the room.

De'Quan sat in the quiet room for five minutes lost in his own thought's until the nurse came back into the room to check on him again, How you feeling?"

"Soar as hell. Where's my brother at?"

The nurse looked over her shoulder, then back to De'Quan and said, "I'm not supposed to be talking to you about anybody else, but I know one of the boys that was in the car with you didn't make it. I don't know if he was a brother of yours, but I am sorry".

De'Quan felt the sincerity in her voice as he nodded and said, "thank you". He let her finish her work, than she disappeared back into the hallway. De'Quan closed his eyes and returned to his own thoughts. She didn't have to tell him who didn't make it; he could feel something inside of him was empty.

Chapter 39

5months later

Dre took Tammy down to her Aunt house in Colombia South Carolina, and they hid out there until Tammy had the baby. They named their baby girl Andrea, and found themselves a small apartment in the country part of the city and kept to themselves, with Tammy finding a job while Dre stayed in the house and took care of the baby.

Dre hooked up with a New York guy he met when he did his bid on Rikers Island and his friend helped Dre move some of the drugs they took from the last robbery. Dre made sure he got De'Quan a lawyer they could trust to keep the communication going between them two, because the police had cut off all other forms of communication Dre had with his family in New York once they found out he was the one who got away that night.

Everybody took it hard when it was known that Ne'Sean died in the car from the crash with the police car. Dre was able to speak to his sister after Ne'Sean's funeral, and Shakia filled her brother in on how Mama K wasn't the same and how she refuse to go see De'Quan while he waited for his trial to start. Shakia went to see De'Quan once a week, but their relationship was full of stress once De'Quan came clean about him hanging out with Melissa to get the information on the place they robbed.

To keep her brother off of the radar Shakia cut ties with him and everybody used De'Quan's lawyer to send Dre messages. Since the night of the incident, nobody had heard from Fat Pee. They knew he wasn't dead, and he wasn't in jail with De'Quan, which led to the rumors flying around, that Fat Pee is working with the police and hiding in some type of witness protection.

Most days De'Quan walked around in a daze as the lost of his brother weighed heavy on his mind and today was no different as he was shipped off to Manhattan Supreme court for a another day of ball pen theory and offers from the DA's office for De'Quan to take a twenty year sentence that didn't stop at that number because the life on the end is what the parole board would be looking at.

De'Quan wanted to take his chances at trial, and the DA's office was all for it. They wanted a judge to sentence De'Quan to a hundred years to life, instead of the sweet deal they were offering him.

When De'Quan arrived at the court building, he was taken to the holding area and placed in a cell by himself. He sat on the bench for an hour lost in his own thoughts until a shadow appeared in front of him, "Hi De'Quan".

De'Quan looked up and was taken aback by who he was looking at standing on the other side of the cell bars, "What are you doing here?"

"I needed to see you", Melissa said.

De'Quan got up from his seat and walked over to the cell bars. He looked her up and down and his eyes rested on the detective badge that hung around her neck and rested in between her chest.

"Yeah, well officer Sanchez, you see me. Fucked up and facing life, so now what", De'Quan said.

"De'Quan I never meant for this to happen. I thought you would only make a purchase or two and that would be it. I'm sorry all of this happen and I'm sorry about your brother", Melissa said seeming truly genuine.

De'Quan thought about her words and knew Melissa was the last person he was going to trust at this time in his life. He took two steps back and said, "Melissa I know you didn't come all the way down here to tell me that. You could have wrote me a letter or sent me card".

Melissa nervously shifted her weight from her right foot to her left foot and unfolded her arms. When she did, Melissa opens up her button up sweater revealing her real reason for coming there.

"I wanted to let you know face to face that I was pregnant. I've been wrestling with thoughts of what to do for months and keeping you out of your baby life is not something can I do. I know you probably don't want anything to do with me, but I know you would want to know about your baby", Melissa said.

De'Quan stared at her stomach, then looked into her eyes and said, "So let me get this straight, you saying that's my baby?"

"Yes De'Quan. You the only one I was sleeping with and a few times we didn't use a condom, so something was bound to happen".

"And you want me to do what…Play daddy from prison. How will your cop friends feel about that?" De'Quan said.

"This has nothing to do with the people I work with. I'm here because I don't want to shut you out of your child life", Melissa said.

"The minute you took me up to that apartment, you shut me out. I lost my brother, and now I'm about to lose my life. I don't think your baby story is going to make any of that better," De'Quan said. He looked down at her stomach one last time then walked back over to the bench and sat down.

A tear rolled down Melissa's cheek, "So that's it?"

"Melissa I have a trial to prepare for and being that you are the DA's leading witness, I don't think it's a good idea for you to be here right now", De'Quan said as he lit up a cigarette.

Melissa stood there in silence for a minute before she wiped her face and said, "Okay De'Quan. You can reach out to me whenever you want. I will never keep you r baby away from you".

De'Quan ignored her and kept his focus on his cigarette. Melissa slowly walked away from the cell feeling defeated. She knew De'Quan was mad at her, but she thought he have a better reception about the baby.

An hour later De'Quan's lawyer showed up at the cell ready to talk strategy, but De'Quan had other plans, "Let me get a pen and paper".

When his lawyer gave it to him, De'Quan wrote a small note and said, "Give this to our friend". His lawyer nodded and stuck the note in his jacket pocket.

Chapter 40

Dre kept his low profile down in South Carolina using side hustles to keep some money coming in, while Tammy worked in a college campus library to keep ligitiment money coming in. Their formula was working for them until Dre got the message from the lawyer.

Tammy sat in their small kitchen feeding their daughter when Dre came in with a sad look on his face. "What's wrong baby?"

Dre sat down at the table and said, "I'm going to New York for a few days".

Tammy never was one to blow up on Dre, but at this moment she felt like smacking him with the baby plate of food, "Are you crazy, for what?"

"I need to take care of something for De'Quan. Tammy you know if it wasn't important I wouldn't go up there, but this is serious, and it might help the case".

Tammy chose her words carefully when she said, "but what if something happens to you, what are we suppose to do?"

Dre got up, kneeled down in front of her, and said, "Trust me baby, nothing is going to happen to me. Nobody is going to know I'm there and nobody is going to see me. I'm going to dip in the city and dip out".

Tammy looked into his eyes and knew she had to trust Dre. She never let her trust for the decisions Dre made affect their bond. If Dre felt this strong about something Tammy had to be the rider that she was and support him again, "Okay Dre. Promise me you going to be careful out there".

Dre kissed her and said, "I promise you and you", then kissed their daughter as the baby squealed with joy from her father affection.

✳✳✳✳✳
___

Melissa felt a funny pain hit her in the stomach as she woke up and rolled out of the bed. She went to the bathroom and when she sat down on the toilet a heavy rush of fluid dropped out of her body scarring her for a second. Then it hit her, this is it. The baby was coming.

Being by herself was never a plan Melissa had for having her first baby, but the circumstances surrounding her pregnancy were complicated and hard for her to talk to anybody about it. Once she reached six months and couldn't hide her growing stomach anymore, Melissa had to tell her family about it, but she kept the baby father identity to herself.

Getting to the hospital was a move she had been planning on her own for a few weeks and now the moment was happening. Melissa slowly dressed herself, and called her friend Suge and told her the baby was coming. Then Melissa grabbed her carry bag and called herself a cab. When Melissa made her way downstairs to the cab the driver was nervous and excited at the same time as he rushed her to Harlem Hospital.

At the hospital, Melissa was helped up to a pre-screening room until the baby began to force its way out into the world.

✳✳✳✳✳

Dre rented a car in New Jersey and used that as his means to move around New York City and follow Melissa whenever she left her house, which was rare being that she was ready to have the baby any day. Sitting in the car was driving Dre crazy, but he knew it will all pay off in the end.

Dre watched Melissa emerge from her building carrying a carry-on bag and looking wore out like she just had a fight. Dre knew that look from watching Tammy go through it when she was in labor with their baby. He immediately sat up and started the car.

Dre followed her to the hospital and watched as two nurses helped Tammy into a wheelchair and rolled her into the hospital. Dre parked the car and looked into the mirror to make sure the make-up he was wearing looked presentable enough where no one will give him a second glace as he moved through the hallways of the hospital.

Harlem Hospital was buzzing with activity at six o'clock in the evening, giving Dre the cover he needed to slide in and make his way up to the paternity unit. As Dre smoothly moved around the unit, he walked past the delivery room Melissa was having her baby in and dipped into a bathroom for an half an hour.

When Dre slipped out of the bathroom, Melissa had a baby boy and the nurses where working on him to get him cleaned up for his first official visit with his new mom. Dre watched from the side as nurses came and went for one reason or another, and when the coast looked, clear enough for him, Dre made his move.

The attending nurse stepped out of the baby holding room to go to the bathroom and Dre slid right into the room and headed straight for the bassinette that said 'Sanchez boy'. Without wasting any time, Dre scooped up the baby and quickly made his way down a side staircase. Just as Dre hit the first floor of the hospital, a commotion broke out in the main lobby causing security to leave their post at the door. Dre walked as fast as he could out of the hospital without looking suspicious and headed for his parked rental car three blocks down. The only thing Dre could think about was thank god the baby was sleeping the whole time.

Dre put the small boy into the car-seat in the back and quickly hopped into the driver seat. He started the car and before he pulled away from the curb Dre took off the nurse hat and wig, he was wearing. He wiped the make-up off of his face, took a quick look in the mirror and pulled out of the parking spot.

Dre jumped on the highway and headed for the George Washington Bridge leaving New York City in his rearview mirror for the last time.

✻✻✻✻✻

When Suge made it to Harlem Hospital, she had to sidestep an altercation in the main lobby and made her way up to the paternity ward without anyone asking her for a visitors pass.

"Excuse me, can you tell me what room is Melissa Sanchez in?" Suge asked a nurse at the nurses' station.

"Oh the new mom, she in room 112".

"Thank you", Suge said and walked into the room hoping to see her girl sitting up feeding the baby by now. Instead she found Melissa sleeping like she just ran the marathon.

"What's up Mame'", Suge said waking her up she gave Melissa a hug and kiss and looked around the room.

"Hey girl, wow I must've fallen asleep. I'm so glad you came so you can meet him", Melissa said feeling worn out.

"I told you I got your back, now where's my god child at", Suge said as she took off her jacket and put her bag down in the chair.

"I don't know. They were supposed to clean him up and weigh him and all that, and then they were going to bring him in.

"Let me see what's going on", Suge said as she went over to the baby holding room and quickly scanned the names on the bassinettes.

"Hi may I help you?" A nurse said as she looked up from putting a bottle in a baby mouth.

"Yes, we were waiting for my god son to be brought in the room", Suge said.

"What's the name?" The nurse asks as she made her way down the aisle.

"Melissa Sanchez", Suge said.

The nurse looked around the room and focused on the empty bassinette in the second aisle, "What in the world?" The nurse rushed over to the bassinette and looked inside of it like she was seeing things.

Suge immediately panicked when she read the name on the empty bassinette, "Oh hell no, where's my god son at bitch!"

"If he's not here, then he's supposed to be in the room with his mother…I don't know", the nurse whined as she nervously looked around the room.

Melissa heard Suge yelling at somebody in the hallway, causing her to climb out of the bed and slowly make her way to the door. "Suge what's going on?"

Suge turned to Melissa with tears sliding down her cheeks and said, "Somebody stole the baby!"

Melissa thought she heard the words wrong, but the look on Suge's face told her brain this was not a test, "What?" was the last thing Melissa said before losing her grip on the I.V. pole and passing out in the doorway.

To Be Continued